Sweet Cherry Ray

Center Point
Large Print

Also by Marcia Lynn McClure and available from Center Point Large Print:

A Crimson Frost
The Prairie Prince
The Bewitching of Amoretta Ipswich
The Secret Bliss of Calliope Ipswich
The Romancing of Evangeline Ipswich
The Tide of the Mermaid Tears
Desert Fire
Midnight Masquerade
Shackles of Honor
Divine Deception
The Horseman

SWEET CHERRY RAY

MARCIA LYNN MCCLURE

CENTER POINT LARGE PRINT
THORNDIKE, MAINE

This Center Point Large Print edition
is published in the year 2024 by arrangement with
Distractions Ink.

Copyright © 2011, 2016 by Marcia Lynn McClure.

All rights reserved.

All character names and personalities in this work of fiction are entirely fictional, created solely in the imagination of the author. Any resemblance to any person living or dead is coincidental.

The text of this Large Print edition is unabridged.
In other aspects, this book may vary
from the original edition.
Printed in the United States of America
on permanent paper sourced using
environmentally responsible foresting methods.
Set in 16-point Times New Roman type.

ISBN: 979-8-89164-300-0

The Library of Congress has cataloged this record
under Library of Congress Control Number: 2024940073

In Loving Memory of My Beloved
Grandmother,
Opal Edith Switzler States
I miss you every day . . .

My everlasting admiration,
gratitude and love . . .
To my husband, Kevin . . .
My inspiration . . .
My heart's desire . . .
The man of my every dream!

CHAPTER ONE

"Riding Old Red bareback with the wind blowing my hair, I drew the trusty peacemaker what had belonged to my pa," Cherry Ray read aloud. She felt her eyes widen with excitement—her heartbeat quickened with delicious anticipation. Rolling over onto her stomach, Cherry was barely conscious of the soft pasture grass beneath her as she continued to read.

"You'll never take me alive, Arizona Bill!" I hollered as a bullet whistled past my right ear. Knowing Old Red would gallop straight and true, I turned in the saddle and took my aim. Squeezing my Colt trigger, I watched as Arizona Bill lurched back in the saddle. His pony slid to a stop, reared, and threw the outlaw to the ground. But my ma didn't raise a fool! I was alone, and Arizona Bill's gang rode hard and fast. If I didn't ride on . . . if'n I stayed to make certain Arizona Bill was dead . . . they'd sure as heck catch me.

Cherry smiled as she paused to listen to a meadowlark whistle from a nearby pine tree. The *Oklahoma Jenny* dime novel in her hands was one of Cherry's true delights. She owned several *Oklahoma Jennys*—much to Mrs. Blakely's disapproval—but she guessed *Oklahoma Jenny and Arizona Bill* was just about her favorite

Oklahoma Jenny adventure. Cherry continued reading.

"Come on, Old Red," I said to my pony. "Let's get on in to Green River before them outlaws find out we done in their boss," Old Red and I understood each other, and the minute I was settled right in the saddle, Old Red bolted. We rode like the wind, Old Red and me. No Arizona Bill or his gang would catch us that day, for Green River was only five miles yonder. Green River meant safety and good, loyal lawmen. Even for being pursued by Arizona and his gang, I couldn't keep my mind off Green River and its handsome sheriff. It'd been three weeks since I'd seen Sheriff Tate. I wondered if the bullet old Doc Whitfield dug outta Sheriff Tate's shoulder . . . the bullet Arizona Bill had put there with his Winchester . . . I wondered if that bullet was still in Sheriff Tate's pocket. I wondered if Sheriff Tate would wink at me the way he'd done so many times in the past. I wondered if he'd wink at me and say, "Hey, there, Jenny. What might ya think about a-marryin' up with me?" I smiled and told Old Red to get to a faster gallop. For Sheriff Tate I would hang up my gun. Me . . . Oklahoma Jenny . . . I'd take to being his wife like fleas take to nippin' a hound! Indeedy I would.

"Cherry? Cherry Ray!" It was Mrs. Blakely. It seemed like Mrs. Blakely was always hollering from the house for Cherry.

Breathing a heavy sigh of disappointment, she closed her tattered copy of *Oklahoma Jenny and Arizona Bill* begrudgingly and raised herself from the fragrant pasture grasses. She placed the book inside a weathered tin box where she kept her Oklahoma Jennys. Closing the lid, she pushed the box into the hollow of a nearby tree.

"Comin', Mrs. Blakely," Cherry called.

"Hurry on, Cherry! Your pa's fixin' to leave," Mrs. Blakely called.

"I'm comin', I'm comin'!" she shouted.

Cherry tied her long brown hair up in a knot at the back of her head as she walked to where her pa was waiting with the wagon.

"Here ya go, girl," Arthur Ray said, handing a weathered hat to his daughter. Cherry climbed up onto the wagon seat beside him.

Pulling the hat onto her head, she said, "Thanks, Pa." Adjusting the hat so it sat low enough to cover her eyebrows, Cherry returned her pa's loving smile.

"That girl needs to be in skirts and petticoats, Arthur," Mrs. Blakely said, wagging a scolding index finger at the man.

"Ain't no need fer Cherry to be draggin' any attention to herself in town these days, Fiona."

Cherry smiled at her pa. Oh, she knew her pa had her dressing in men's blue jeans, boots, shirts, and hats in order to keep her from being noticed by the likes of Black Jack Haley and his outfit. Still, she liked to imagine her own pa was like Oklahoma Jenny's—allowing her to run as untamed and free as any wild mustang.

"She's a woman, Arthur," Mrs. Blakely reminded.

Cherry sighed and rolled her eyes. Oh, she loved Mrs. Blakely well enough, and she was thankful her pa had found such a grandmotherly old woman to cook for the ranch hands and help with the house. White-haired, leathery, and as scrawny as any old polecat, Mrs. Blakely was a hard woman. Yet hard women were the ones that survived hard living. Cherry stared at Mrs. Blakely for a moment. Yep—she could well imagine Fiona Blakely shooting rabbits for supper while riding a barebacked pony. For all she knew, Fiona Blakely had been the inspiration for the Oklahoma Jenny dime novels. Therefore, Cherry always convinced herself to be patient with Mrs. Blakely. After all, every old woman had once been a young one.

"And she needs to be dressin' like a woman," Mrs. Blakely added.

"She does," Arthur Ray said. "Every Sunday."

"We'll see ya fer supper, Mrs. Blakely," Cherry said as her pa slapped the lines at the backs of the team.

The team lurched forward, and Cherry smiled as Mrs. Blakely waved, still shaking her head.

"She's right, ya know. Ya are a woman, Cherry."

She shrugged. "I know it. But yer the one who—"

"I know it," he interrupted. "And as long as Black Jack and his boys are a-ridin' through town every week or so . . . well, I'd just as soon have you blendin' in. There's plenty of fillies in town those ol' boys sent to sobbin' with their outlaw words and ways. You just keep blendin' in all easy and such—for now—for yer old pa's sake."

"You bet," Cherry said, smiling brightly as she hooked her arm in his and rested her head on her pa's strong shoulder.

Cherry sighed, contented for a moment. Still, as she glanced down to the pinned-up trouser leg hanging off the wagon seat, her smile faded. Having lost his left leg in the war between the states, it was quite a miracle that Arthur Ray had built such a successful cattle ranch. Cherry's mind wandered to the pair of crutches she knew were in the wagon bed behind them. A little whisper of doubt and insecurity pricked at her heart. Arthur Ray was growing weaker and weaker. Every year his dark hair seemed sprinkled with more gray, and his using his crutches appeared more and more difficult.

Cherry's mother had died when she was a baby, leaving her cherished pa as the only parent she had ever known. Her pa had never remarried; thus Cherry was without any siblings for company. At times, a dark, foreboding feeling would envelop Cherry's heart—a fear of losing her pa, of being left all alone in the world. Yet she always managed to chase the bad feelings away and linger on the good. Mrs. Blakely said she was "an eternal optimist." It always bothered her—the way Mrs. Blakely said it—as if it were a bad thing. Well, it wasn't! Why not see the good in everything? What benefit was there in walking around with a scowl and always expecting things to go wrong all the time? Nope. For Cherry Ray, life was good, exciting, one big adventure.

"Seems Black Jack ain't been in town for near two weeks," Arthur said.

"So I hear."

"Wonder what he's been up to."

"May be he's moved on," she answered. "Mighta found some other town to linger in between robbin's and killin's."

Arthur Ray shook his head. "Naw," he mumbled. "More'n likely he's hidin' out a bit. Some old boys robbed a bank in San Antone, and I'm guessing it was Black Jack and his bunch."

"Did they kill anybody this time?"

"Yep. Two deputies and a Texas Ranger—way I heard it anyway," he said.

Cherry shivered as a chill ran the length of her spine. She'd seen Black Jack Haley and his boys plenty of times in town. Heck, several times she'd even exchanged a "howdy" with him. Still, everybody knew there were twenty notches on his pistol—one notch for each man he'd murdered. Cherry wondered if Black Jack was hiding out somewhere adding more notches.

"Do ya think anybody will ever catch him, Pa? Will anybody ever get him to jail or hung?"

Arthur Ray shook his head. "If'n I was younger and still had two good legs about me, I'd do it myself for sure. But the lawmen in this town are cowards. It's a wonder there's any order at all. Why, when I was rangerin', we'd a hung him high by now. Lawmen are gettin' too soft these days—too fearful."

"I heard someone say Black Jack was born in Blue Water and that's why he leaves us all purty well alone."

Arthur chuckled and looked to his daughter. "Who told ya that, girl?"

"Ol' Lefty."

"Lefty Pierce? I swear, Cherry—I don't know what ya see in that old feller. He's as ornery as a mule and near as ugly."

"But he was young once, Pa . . . and he knows a heap about things 'round here in Blue Water," Cherry explained.

Arthur chuckled. "That he does," he said. "That he does. He's right about Black Jack too. That old outlaw was born and raised right here in Blue Water. Took to robbin' trains and banks after all his kin died, a-leavin' him orphaned. Weren't enough money in cowboyin' . . . and it's too hard a work for a devil like Black Jack."

"Well, I'm just glad he leaves us all be," she said. "Wouldn't do to have an outlaw hangin' 'round that didn't feel some sort of loyalty to the town."

"Oh, but outlaws is outlaws for a reason, Cherry. There ain't no trustin' 'em. They'll turn on ya quicker'n any rattler. That's why you and me—that's why we just lay low whenever Black Jack and his boys are hangin' 'round here."

Cherry looked at her pa. His brow was furrowed with a deep frown, his face too stern and red for his insides to be calm.

"It gives ya fits, don't it, Pa?" she asked. "Not bein' able to take ol' Black Jack and his boys to jail."

"It does at that, Cherry," he admitted. "And if it weren't for worryin' over what might happen to you—well, I'm still a better shot than any of them old boys. I'd drop Black Jack myself—if I was one hundred percent sure that I still could."

"Someone will drop him one day, Pa. Don't you worry," she said, smiling at her pa and tucking his hair behind his ear. "You need a trim. Yer lookin' about like that ol' shaggy mutt we used to have when I was little."

"Ol' Nobby?" he chuckled. "Well if'n yer thinkin' I'm lookin' like Ol' Nobby, then I had better pay a visit to the barber while I'm in town."

Cherry smiled and inhaled a deep breath. Oh, how delicious the day smelled! The warm breeze through the pasture grass lent such a fragrance to the air—the fragrance of heaven itself! The sun shone bright and hot, and Cherry wished she could ride without her hat. She grimaced at the feel of the perspiration collecting on her forehead. She hated the old hat her pa had given her to wear. How she wished she could dress up in pretty dresses, hot-iron her hair into soft curls the way the other young women in town did. Still, she thought of the twenty notches on Black Jack's pistol and sighed, resigned to remaining as unnoticeable as possible.

Blue Water seemed to be bustling more than usual. Of course, Blue Water always did bustle when Black Jack and his boys were away. It seemed folks' hearts were lighter and felt more like doing when the outlaws weren't in town.

As her pa drove the wagon down the main street, Cherry smiled and waved when Billy Parker waved both hands at her with delight.

"Ma's got a new litter of kittens in the shed," the tall, gangly young man called. "Ya want I should save ya one, Cherry?"

She nodded, but her pa answered, "Cherry don't need no more animals, Billy. She's already got a smelly dog and one plum cantankerous ol' tom out in the barn."

"Well, sure he's cantankerous, Mr. Ray," Billy said. "He's in need of a wife to keep him company."

"No more varmints, Billy. Especially cats," Arthur said.

But as her pa looked away, Cherry smiled and nodded at the boy.

"Save me a female," she mouthed to him.

"Sure thing," Billy mouthed back, smiling and nodding his head with assurance.

"Now don't ya go draggin' one of Parker's cats on home, Cherry Ray," her pa chuckled. "Stanky don't like cats the way it is."

"Well, Stanky will just hafta learn to," she said. "Besides, that ol' dog wouldn't even have a home if Lefty Pierce hadn't a given him to me. Ol' Lefty was gonna drown him in the creek! And don't try to tell me you don't love him, Pa. He's the best cattle dog in the county!"

Arthur smiled and nodded. "That he is . . . even if he does only have three legs."

Arthur halted the team in front of the general store.

"Hey there, Arthur," Otis Hirsch greeted. Tipping his hat to Cherry, Otis reached into the wagon and pulled out Arthur's crutches. "I got them books in ya ordered last month."

"Dang time," Arthur said as he scooted across

the wagon seat and hopped out of the wagon.

"Yeah, they took a piece a time gettin' here," Otis said as he handed Arthur his crutches.

"Cherry!" Billy Parker called. Cherry smiled as she saw the young man and his younger brother and sister run up behind the wagon. "Ya gotta come with us, Cherry," Billy said.

"Yeah!" his sister Laura added. "We found somethin' you just gotta see!"

"What's that?" Cherry asked.

"A dried-up ol' coyote," Billy's younger brother, Pocket, answered.

"Dried up?" she asked.

"We figure it musta crawled into that ol' abandoned shed just outside of town and died and just dried up," Billy explained. "It's still got hair on it and skin and everything, but it's as dried up as an old apple core."

As Laura took Cherry's hand and began tugging on it, Arthur called, "Where ya off to, Cherry? I don't want to linger too long."

"Just goin' over to see a dried-up coyote, Pa," she answered. "I won't be long."

She giggled as she heard Mr. Hirsch ask, "A dried-up coyote?"

"How long do ya think it's been in there, Cherry? How long do ya think it would take to dry up a coyote?" Billy asked.

Billy Parker was what Cherry's pa called "an inquisitive youth." Billy was forever searching for adventure, entertainment, or anything else to keep his mind and body occupied. He was five years younger than Cherry but a handsome enough lad. Cherry figured Billy Parker would have broken every silly girl's heart in Blue Water by the time he was twenty. Yet, to Cherry, Billy was like the little brother she'd never had. She was fond of Pocket and Laura too. They were good kids.

"I wouldn't know," Cherry said as she followed the children to the abandoned shed outside of town. "Seems to me it would take awhile for it to dry all the way up though."

"There weren't much rain last summer," Pocket said.

"Maybe it was sick or wounded or somethin' and was just lookin' for a place to heal up," Laura said.

"Maybe," she said.

The shed outside of town was hardly a shed at all. As Cherry followed the children inside, she smiled. She'd wandered into the old shed a time or two when she had been a child. Overgrown with honeysuckle and void of one wall, the shed had always interested her. Who had owned it? Who had owned the piano that had once resided in the old mouse-ridden piano crate inside the shed?

"Right there," Billy said, pointing to a far

corner of the shed near the old piano crate. "See it?"

"It's a coyote, ain't it?" Pocket asked.

Cherry frowned and squinted, trying to see into the darkened corner. She could see the dried-out carcass of an animal all right. Curled up as if it had just gone to sleep, the animal's body was completely dehydrated—mummified in a manner. Patches of fur still clung to the leathered skin. The skin had dried and now shrunk against the bones until the shape and outline of ribs, the skull, and every other part of the skeleton were visible. The flesh of the animal had receded from its mouth, and the revealed teeth made the pitiful creature appear as if it still snarled in death.

"I do wonder how long it's been there," Cherry mused.

"Quite awhile, I'd say," Billy mumbled.

Cherry felt her eyes widen. The carcass intrigued her.

"Hand me that ol' pitchfork in the corner there, Billy," she said.

"Whatcha plannin', Cherry?" Pocket asked.

"Let's get it out of here to where we can see it better," she explained.

The Parker kids gathered around her as she slipped the pitchfork under the animal's dried carcass. The dead thing easily lifted, and she carried it out into the sunshine.

"Would ya look at that," Laura exclaimed in an awed whisper.

"Yeah," Cherry breathed as she studied the animal's carcass.

In the brighter light of the full sunshine, she could see more fur clung to the dried skin than she had originally thought. She could also see that the flesh of the eyelids had receded as well, revealing two empty eye sockets.

"It's givin' me the willies!" Pocket whispered.

"I ain't sure this is a coyote," Cherry said. "It just looks a little . . . different somehow."

"Let's take it back to town and ask yer pa, Cherry," Billy suggested. "He might know for sure."

"Yeah. He might."

"I wonder what happened," Laura sighed as the children and Cherry walked back to town. Cherry carefully balanced the dead animal carcass on the old pitchfork. It was a curious find. It made a body wonder about what else heat and dry air could do.

"I don't see any wounds," Billy said.

"Maybe it just took sick," Pocket suggested.

"Maybe it was female, and she run in there to have her pups," Billy said.

"Oh no!" Laura gasped, covering her mouth with her hands. "What if she had pups and then she died? Her pups would've died too!"

"Oh, I'm sure there weren't any pups. We didn't

find any," Cherry said. She saw the tears welling in Laura's eyes, and her own heart felt the need to offer comfort. Still, a lump caught in Cherry's own throat at the thought there may have been a litter of coyote pups that wandered off and were eaten by hawks or the like.

"Well, what in tarnation is that?"

Arthur Ray looked up to see Otis gazing off toward the edge of town. Looking for himself, he chuckled when he saw Cherry carrying a pitchfork and three children following after her like she were their ma. He squinted into the sun, trying to make out what was on the pitchfork, but he couldn't.

"Looks like Cherry's been up to somethin'," Arthur chuckled.

He smiled. Oh, how he loved his beautiful daughter! And oh, how he worried for her. At nineteen, Cherry Ray was the loveliest girl in Blue Water. It had become harder and harder to hide the fact, yet Arthur kept trying. He knew the likes of Black Jack Haley and his boys— knew how they fancied a pretty face. It's why he'd been dressing Cherry like a boy the past few years—to keep her pretty face, soft brown hair, and sparkling blue eyes from being noticed. Oh, in his day, Arthur Ray had been a man to contend with. Riding as a Texas Ranger before the war, there wasn't an outlaw or criminal that didn't fear the name of Arthur Ray. Yet without his leg, he knew he was easy prey—that his daughter was easy prey because of it. And so he'd decided to hide Cherry—hide her until the day someone shot Black Jack Haley between the eyes and made Blue Water safe again.

"Pa!" Cherry called as she and the Parkers approached her pa and Mr. Hirsch. "Pa! Look what the kids found out in the old shed outside a town."

"Looks to be a dead coyote," Mr. Hirsch said as Cherry gently laid the animal carcass on the ground.

"Nope," Arthur mumbled.

Cherry watched with pride as her pa's eyes narrowed.

He studied the animal for a moment and then said, "That there's a red wolf."

"A wolf!" Pocket exclaimed.

"Yep," Arthur said. "Probably a purty mean ol' boy in his day too. Look at the size of them paws."

"But it's so small," Billy said. "I thought wolves were bigger."

"Oh, this one was bigger, boy," Arthur said. "But he's all shriveled and dried up now. Ain't much left to him."

"A wolf!" Laura whispered in awe.

"Pa," Cherry began, "why do ya think he'd be out in that old shed?"

Her pa started to answer but was interrupted as Remmy Cooper rode up, reining in before them.

"There's a rider comin'!" he exclaimed. Remmy Cooper was a hired hand on a nearby ranch. Cherry had always fancied him as handsome, and she smiled as he looked at her.

"Black Jack?" Mr. Hirsch asked.

"Nope," Remmy said. "Ain't one of his boys neither. But he looks the sort that might join up with an outlaw."

"Better ride on and tell Sheriff Gibbs, Remmy," Arthur said. "Not that it will help none," he added under his breath.

Remmy nodded and rode off toward the sheriff's office and jail.

"I see him!" Billy exclaimed. Cherry looked to see Billy leaning over and looking down the road. "Here he comes! Here he comes! And he looks like a bad one too."

Cherry glanced at her pa, who frowned and slightly shook his head. Still, she couldn't help herself, and she leaned over and looked down the road herself.

She could see the rider and his horse—a large buckskin stallion. As he rode nearer, she studied his white shirt, black flat-brimmed hat, and double-breasted vest. Ever nearer he rode, and she fancied his pants were almost the same color as his horse, with silver buttons running down the outer leg. Cherry had seen a similar manner of dress before—on the Mexican vaqueros that often worked for her pa in the fall.

"Cherry," her pa scolded in a whisper as the stranger neared them.

She straightened and blushed, embarrassed by being as impolite in her staring as the other townsfolk were in theirs. It seemed everyone had stopped whatever they had been doing to walk out to the street and watch the stranger ride in.

No one spoke. The only sound was that of the breeze, a falcon's cry overhead, and the rhythm of the rider's horse as it slowed to a trot. Everyone watched as the stranger rode closer and closer. Cherry felt her own heart pounding wildly within her bosom. Was the rider a new outlaw come to join Black Jack's boys? Or was he an outlaw to himself—perhaps come to Blue Water to challenge Jack?

The rider's horse slowed its pace to a steady walk. Cherry squeezed Laura's hand tightly and dropped her gaze as he reined his horse in directly before them.

"Howdy there, stranger," Cherry heard her pa say. Cherry could not find the courage to look up at the stranger. As much as she claimed to be fearless, she was, in truth, fearful of any outlaw.

"Howdy," the stranger said.

The sound of his voice was like magic—forcing anyone to want to see what its owner looked like. Instantly, Cherry looked up to the stranger. She felt her jaw go slack, her mouth drop open in astonishment. The stranger was far more handsome than any man Cherry had ever seen—even Remmy Cooper!

"What can we do for ya?" Arthur Ray asked.

Sitting astride the buckskin, tall and straight in the saddle, the stranger owned a fine set of broad shoulders, a slightly cleft chin, and a strong, squared jaw. Dark hair and even darker eyes lent him an imposing, threatening appearance, and she knew at once—this was no man to meddle with.

"Lookin' for a room," the stranger said.

She was nearly paralyzed with intimidation as the stranger glanced at her for a moment. Immediately, his gaze returned to her, his eyes narrowing, his brow puckering into a frown. He studied her quickly from head to toe, his frown deepening as he visually noted the dried-up wolf carcass at her feet.

"There's a boardin' house yonder," Arthur said, nodding in the direction of the boarding house.

"Thank ya kindly, mister," the stranger said, nodding to Arthur. His attention then returned to Cherry. The frown on his brow softened but did not completely disappear as he touched the brim of his hat and said, "Um . . . ma'am." He clicked his tongue, and his horse moved on down the road.

For the first time since her pa had insisted

she dress like a man, Cherry Ray resented it. Humiliation the like she had never known was washing over her. She thought of all the saloon girls across the street at the saloon. Hussies or not, at least they looked like women! She doubted the stranger would have crinkled his brow in disgust at them.

"I ain't never seen an outlaw as handsome as that before," Laura said.

"Well, I think it's plum awful that ya've seen any outlaws at all, Laura," Arthur said.

Cherry straightened then. Handsome or not, it was obvious the man meant no good. She sighed, relieved in the knowledge that the man was a drifter or an outlaw and not someone she might be interested in attracting attention from. Let him have the girlie saloon girls—if that's where his trail led.

"Now," Arthur began, "tell me a might more about this here wolf, Billy."

Glancing down the road to where the rider had reined in before the boarding house, Cherry silently scolded her heart for its wild hammering. Another outlaw had ridden to Blue Water. No good could come from it, she knew. Yet Cherry Ray thought she better understood, in that moment, how Oklahoma Jenny's sister, Pearl, had once been charmed out of her egg and milk money by a handsome drifter—especially if he looked anything like the stranger on the buckskin.

• • •

"It's all we're needin' 'round here," Arthur grumbled as he drove the wagon back toward the ranch.

"Ya mean the stranger in town today?" Cherry asked. She hadn't been able to think of anything else since she'd seen him—the handsome stranger with the vaquero's pants and flat-brimmed hat. It stood to reason her pa, being the retired Texas Ranger he was, had been thinking of him too.

"Yep," he said.

"Well, maybe he'll just ride on through. Maybe he ain't here to join up with Black Jack."

"Oh, he ain't! A man like that ain't here to join up with another outlaw. No indeedy," he said. "Not lookin' like that and with so much strength about him. Nope. I reckon he's more'n likely here to take ol' Jack down and gather up his boys for his own reasons."

Cherry exhaled a heavy sigh, trying to rid herself of the butterflies flapping in her stomach every time she thought of the stranger. Glancing back into the wagon bed, she frowned.

"Do ya think Ol' Red will weather the trip home in one piece?" she asked.

She smiled when she heard the wonderful sound of her pa's chuckle.

"I'm sure he will . . . but heck if I know what yer gonna do with a dried-up ol' wolf when we get there. It's bad enough yer always draggin' the live varmints home. Now yer draggin' home the dead ones too."

She laughed. "I guess I am a little strange. Still, I promised the Parker kids I'd make sure he had a nice place by the hearth . . . cool in the summer and warm in the winter."

"Mrs. Blakely will have a hen-peckin' fit, that's for sure," Arthur said.

Cherry looked to the old, dead wolf lying in the back of the wagon. Old Red had once lived—free, fierce, and wild. If he'd been too strong for the wind, rain, and time to take him, then he deserved to have a comfortable place to rest until he did turn to dust.

"I think he was a might fine wolf once, Pa," she said. Glancing down at her pa's empty trouser leg, she put her arms around his still broad shoulders. "He deserves more than to rot away in a dark, lonesome corner of some old shed."

Her pa smiled and patted Cherry's knee.

"Well, when ya put it to me like that, it makes more sense than just about anythin'," he said.

Cherry closed her eyes. She thought of the beauty of the day, of the old dried-up wolf in the back of the wagon, and of her pa. What a sight he must've been in his rangering days. Tall, strong, and faster with a pistol than any Texas Ranger that had ever lived, Arthur Ray was a legend. Yet, proud as she was of tales of Ranger Arthur Ray,

Cherry was glad her pa's law-keeping days were over. Though she often wished he was still strong enough to rid Blue Water of its local outlaw, Black Jack, she was glad it wouldn't be her pa who might one day put a bullet between the eyes of the handsome stranger back in town.

CHAPTER TWO

"Well, all I know is he ain't a-sayin' nothin' to nobody," Lefty Pierce said.

Cherry watched as Mrs. Blakely handed Old Lefty a fork and said, "Sounds like a bad one to me."

"Thank ya kindly, Fiona," Lefty said, plunging the fork into the piece of cake on the plate in front of him.

Cherry smiled, delighted by the old man's white hair and otherwise weathered appearance.

"Yer welcome, Lefty," Mrs. Blakely said, forcing a smile at the roughened-up old cowpoke. "We surely don't need another body joinin' up with Black Jack."

"Pa don't think he's plannin' on joinin' Jack and his boys," Cherry said.

Lefty looked to Cherry, then to Arthur. "That right, Arthur?" he asked. "You think that stranger in town is plannin' on startin' up his own gang a outlaws?"

Cherry looked to her pa in time to see him shrug his shoulders.

"The man don't look like the followin' kind," he said. "Looks more like the leadin' kind. And that Colt he's wearin'—wears it low on his hip like a gunman. Men like that, they either ride alone or do the leadin'."

"So why ya think he's in Blue Water?" Lefty asked.

Again, Arthur Ray shrugged his shoulders. "I don't rightly know fer certain, but I do think trouble's a-comin' . . . one way or the other."

"Maybe a shoot out, like over in Tombstone," Cherry suggested. "Only with one outlaw gunnin' down another instead of lawmen doin' the gunnin'?"

"Maybe," Arthur agreed. "I'd hate to see the folks in Blue Water a-standin' in the middle of two outlaws a-fightin' fer territory though."

"Well, why don't somebody just walk up and ask him?" Cherry asked. "Why is everybody all fearful of him anyway? We all talk to Black Jack like he's just a regular feller . . . and he's got twenty notches on his gun. Why don't we just treat the stranger the same way?"

"Jack holds some sorta loyalty to Blue Water and its folks, Cherry," Arthur explained. "An outlaw who don't . . . well, he might not be as comfortable with folks knowin' his business."

"Well, I ain't afraid to ask him. I ain't afraid to ask him nothin'."

"Don't you go nowhere near that outlaw, Cherry!" Arthur growled, wagging a scolding index finger at her. "We don't know nothin' about him. Besides . . . it seems to me you already caught his eye with that dang dead wolf a-layin' at yer feet when he rode in yesterday."

"That the one over there in the corner?" Lefty asked, winking at Cherry.

Cherry liked Lefty Pierce. He was full of stuff and vinegar. Lefty always had a tale to tell too.

"Yes," Fiona sighed. "That would be the one over there in the corner. I don't know how I'm expected to keep this house clean with Cherry a-draggin' in every rotten thing she finds."

But Arthur wasn't so easily distracted. "You stay outta that ol' boy's way, Cherry," he said. "You hear me?"

"Yes, Pa," she said—but she didn't mean it. Nope. Cherry Ray had thought of nothing else in the world but the stranger in the vaquero's pants since the moment he'd ridden into town the day before. He looked like an outlaw—sure enough he did. Still, there was such a feeling of mystery in Cherry's mind; she was intrigued like she never had been before. She meant to find out more about the stranger—with or without her pa's permission.

"That there is the best cake I ever ate, Fiona," Lefty said.

Cherry giggled when she noticed the blush accompanying Fiona's smile.

"Thank you, Lefty Pierce," Fiona said. "Would ya like another piece?"

There was a knock on the front door, and Mrs. Blakely rolled her eyes. "Who could that be?" she grumbled as she started for the door. "Who in tarnation would be droppin' by at supper time?"

"I can only think of one feller rude enough for that," Lefty began, "but I'm already here." He chuckled and winked at Cherry.

"Well, what are you children doin' out and about so late in the afternoon?" Cherry heard Mrs. Blakely ask.

It was Billy Parker's voice that answered. "We was just wonderin' if we could talk to Cherry for a minute," Billy said.

"Can I be excused, Pa?" She figured the Parker kids might want to see where she'd put the old red wolf to rest. Still, she'd rather they waited until her pa had finished his supper and conversation with Lefty.

"Yes," Arthur said with a wink. "But don't you go leadin' them children into mischief. You hear me?"

"Pa . . . now you know I stay clear of mischief these days," she said, pushing her chair away from the table. "I ain't been in mischief for months!"

"And that's exactly what's got me worried, girl. Seems like it's a ripe time for you to step in somethin'."

"They probably just want to see the old wolf, Pa," Cherry said. "I'll sit out on the porch with 'em a while and wait until ya finished with supper."

"Now, yer a young lady, Cherry," Mrs. Blakely

reminded as she stepped out onto the porch. "And ya need to remember to start actin' more like one."

"Yes, ma'am," she mumbled. She was tired of Mrs. Blakely's constant nagging. What? Did Mrs. Blakely really think she preferred to dress like a boy? Didn't the old nag understand she was only doing what her pa wanted?

"Now you children let these men finish up their supper. They've worked a hard day," Mrs. Blakely said.

Cherry breathed an irritated sigh as Mrs. Blakely closed the door, leaving her alone with the Parker kids.

"How long they gonna be?" Billy asked.

"Not long. Unless they get to talkin' too deep. Then it could be hours."

"Then let's hope they get to talkin' deep," Pocket said.

Cherry frowned, yet the back of her neck prickled with delightful anticipation—as if certain mischief lurked just around the bend.

"Why's that?" she asked.

"'Cause that new outlaw is sittin' in the crick yonder . . . neked as a jaybird!" Laura whispered with a giggle.

"The one that rode in yesterday?" Cherry asked. Oh, she tried to squelch the wonderful and very familiar wave of mischief rinsing through her—but she couldn't.

"That's him," Billy said.

"And we got Pa's spyglass with us," Pocket offered in a whisper.

Cherry studied the twinkles in Billy's eyes—in Pocket's and Laura's. She knew she shouldn't encourage them toward tomfoolery—she knew it.

Still, she felt a smile spread across her face as she said, "Then what are we waitin' for?"

"See there, Cherry?" Billy asked in a whisper. "If he ain't got his britches on, then I suspect he ain't got his gun on neither."

"Let me take a look," she said, holding out her hand.

Billy promptly placed the old spyglass in her palm.

"Careful, Cherry," Pocket said. "If Pa finds out we done took his spyglass without askin', he'll tan our hides good."

"Shhh," Cherry whispered from their hiding place behind a big boulder.

Closing her left eye, she peered through the spyglass. She could see the stranger there in the creek. He was sitting in the water, leaning back against a big rock. Cherry felt her mouth drop open as she looked through the spyglass at the stranger. Bare from at least the waist up, the muscles in his broad shoulders and upper body were like nothing Cherry Ray had ever seen! As he tucked his hands behind his head, seeming to study the clouds in the sky for a moment, she smiled. It seemed she and the Parker kids had caught the handsome stranger completely off his guard.

"Yep," Cherry whispered. "He's as neked as the day he was born." She smiled, delighted by seeing the stranger in such a vulnerable situation. "I can see his gun too. It's holstered and lyin' there with his clothes on the crick bank."

"Just like Black Jack," Billy said. "He's always dippin' in the crick this time a year."

"That he is," Cherry whispered, handing the spyglass to Billy when he held out his hand.

"Must be somethin' outlaws like to do," Laura whispered.

"I suspect most folks—well, fellers anyway—like to bath in the crick now and again," Cherry answered.

"Yep," Billy said as he peered through the spyglass at the stranger. "Our pa's always strippin' down to his nothin's and dippin' in the crick up by our house."

Pocket took the spyglass from Billy and pointed it at the stranger. "What do ya think he's up to, Cherry?" the younger boy asked. "Why do ya think he rode into Blue Water?"

Pocket handed the spyglass to Cherry. Closing one eye, she again peered through the glass at the stranger. He still sat in the creek, entirely unaware he was being spied on by four mischief-makers.

"Pa thinks he's come here to challenge Black Jack for some territory," she said. "But I just don't know."

"Well, he ain't ugly like Black Jack," Laura said.

"Lots of women think Black Jack's awful handsome," Cherry said.

"Women like Pinky Chitter?" Laura asked.

Pinky Chitter was the head girl at the saloon in Blue Water. She was Black Jack's "woman"—or so she claimed.

"All types of women," Cherry said.

"Do you think Black Jack is handsome?" Laura asked.

Cherry continued to gaze through the spyglass at the stranger. Was he asleep? He looked it now.

"Not near as handsome as this ol' boy sittin' in the crick," she whispered.

Suddenly, Cherry gasped and ducked down. The stranger had looked up—looked in their direction. Her heart was pounding like a herd of stampeding cattle was pinned up inside her. If the stranger saw them—if he found out she and the Parker kids had been spying on him . . .

"Here," she said, handing the spyglass back to Billy. "You all get on home. We better not linger too long here."

"We're safe enough, Cherry," Billy said. "That

ol' boy don't even have his britches on. He can't do much to us from sittin' in the middle of the crick without his britches on."

"Maybe . . . but I don't think we oughta wait around to find out. Now get on home before yer pa finds out ya took his spyglass."

"All right, Cherry. All right," Billy grumbled.

"But come and fetch me if this stranger does anything else interesting," she said.

"You bet," Billy said, smiling.

Cherry smiled as well—watching affectionately as Billy, Pocket, and Laura hurried off toward home.

Inhaling a deep breath of courage, she slowly peeked over the boulder back toward the creek. She held her breath, her heart suddenly racing. The stranger was gone! He no longer sat lazily bathing in the creek.

Cherry glanced about quickly. Where was he? Had he simply finished his bath and taken himself back to town?

"It ain't polite to spy on folks when they're bathin'."

Cherry let out an involuntary squeal as she leapt to her feet and spun around to find the handsome stranger standing directly behind her. She gasped, suddenly breathless, as she quickly noted he wore only his pants and gun belt. She glanced at the Colt at his hip, hoping he wasn't about to add a notch to it at her expense.

"Whatcha got to say fer yerself?" he asked.

But she was still speechless. He was even larger up close than he appeared from a distance. As water dripped from his wet hair onto his chest, trickling in rivulets over the muscles of his torso, Cherry began to panic.

At last, she stammered, "Are—are ya gonna shoot me, mister?"

She watched as the stranger's dark eyes narrowed. "I ain't decided yet. I reckon it'll depend on whether you were plannin' on shootin' *me* . . . or whether you were just interested in seein' me neked."

Cherry shook her head and stammered, "I ain't never shot nobody, mister. I ain't even armed."

He studied her for a moment—from head to toe.

"Well, if ya weren't gonna shoot me, then ya must've just wanted to see me—" he began.

"I didn't want to see nothin', mister!" she exclaimed. "I-I mean . . . I didn't see nothin' more'n I see right now."

"Really," he stated more than asked.

She swallowed the lump in her throat as he raked one hand through his wet hair and brushed the rivulets of water off his chest.

"Well? What do ya think?" he asked.

"About what, mister?"

"About what ya see right now," he asked, brushing more water from his chest.

"I . . . I ain't really thinkin' on any of it, mister," she lied. And what a lie it was! In truth, Cherry Ray hadn't ever seen anything the like of the stranger's bare chest and stomach! None of the cowboys working on her pa's ranch looked anything like the stranger did—with or without clothes.

She looked up to his handsome face when she heard him chuckle.

"Well, ya ought not to be spyin' on men when they're bathin'," he said. "And ya ought not be out here alone."

Cherry's fear and anxiety began to trade hands with confidence and indignation. He'd smiled and even chuckled—not the behavior of a man who meant to shoot her in cold blood. And furthermore, who was he to be telling her what she could and couldn't do, where she could or couldn't be?

"I come out here all the time," she told him. "This crick runs right over my pa's ranch."

"May be that it does," he said, his eyes narrowing once more. "Still don't mean it's smart to be wanderin' about when there's so many outlaws roamin' free in Blue Water."

"Are you an outlaw?" The question was out of her mouth before she could even think of stopping it. "You here to join up with Black Jack and his boys?"

"You run off at the mouth all too easy," the

stranger said. "That'll get ya in trouble if yer not careful."

"Everyone thinks yer here to join up with Black Jack. Everyone but my pa," she said, paying no heed to his warning—though she was momentarily distracted by the deep brown of his eyes and the way his lips barely moved when he spoke.

"Is that so?" he asked.

"Yep. Pa says you don't look like a joinin'-up man. He says yer more'n likely a gunman with yer own business to be around."

"Well, it would be yer pa that's right," he said. "And it would be yer pa that oughta keep a better eye on you."

"I'm fine on my own," she said. Her defiance had been tickled now, and she was determined to stand her ground. She'd lived in Blue Water long enough, seen Black Jack Haley gun down enough men, to know that if the stranger was going to shoot her, he'd have done it by now. If his intentions were anything else along the lines of bad, he'd have done that by now too.

"Well, I will say this," he began, looking from her hat to her boots and back again. "Yer a might pretty boy."

A teasing smile spread across his far too handsome face. Cherry tried not to notice the flutter in her heart threatening to dampen her flaring temper. He was making fun of her, teasing her about being dressed like a boy! Deep inside she felt hurt, angry that she stood before the handsome stranger dressed like an adolescent boy instead of the feminine young woman she was. For a moment, she was angry with her pa—angry with him for insisting she dress like she did. Yet he cared for her, worried for her well-being, and she knew that too. She wondered if the man before her would be treating her like a child if she weren't dressed like one. Still, she wondered if her attire had kept her safe. Would his intentions toward her have been more threatening—more along the lines of those of an outlaw—had she been wearing her Sunday pink instead of trousers and a man's shirt?

Suddenly, she wondered, in saying she was a pretty boy, was he implying she was pretty or that she looked like a boy?

"Yep," he said as her silence drug on, "a mighty pretty boy indeed." He reached down and picked a foxtail from amid the grass. Cherry watched as he placed it in his mouth and began chewing on it.

"Well, ain't that a coincidence," she said, forcing a smile and fortifying her courage. "'Cause yer mighty pretty yerself. Them girls over at the saloon oughta be linin' up to—"

"Ya ought not to be a flirtin' with strangers, girl," he said then. "Especially gunmen and outlaws. You might find yerself—"

"I ain't flirtin', mister!" she interrupted. Cherry

grit her teeth, determined not to be intimidated when he took hold of her arm.

"Ain't you scared of me?" he growled. " 'Cause ya oughta be."

"I ain't scared of nothin'," Cherry said. It was a lie, of course. But who did he think he was? She'd show him—yes, sirree, she would! Cherry would show him she was as strong as any man he'd ever known. She wasn't about to back down! Oklahoma Jenny never backed down—and neither would Cherry Ray.

"Nothin'?"

"Nope," she said, straightening her shoulders.

He chuckled. "Oh, yer scared of somethin'," he said.

"I ain't," Cherry assured him. She felt her eyes narrow. Oh, how he tugged her temper! "I ain't scared of Black Jack, his boys, or you."

"Well, then yer as ignorant as ya are a pretty boy," the stranger said. His smile faded a bit, and though she would never admit it to him, the fact made her nervous.

"I'm as good as any man with a rifle," she said. "Or a pistol for that matter. A horse too."

"Are ya a fast runner?"

She frowned. "Yeah."

The stranger's eyes narrowed then. "Well, ya better be."

"Why?"

"You think yer pa keeps ya dressed like that

'cause he likes to see his pretty little girl runnin' around lookin' like a feller?"

"H-he just worries, that's all."

"And do ya know what he worries about?"

Cherry felt her heart begin to pound with a familiar anxiety—an anxiety she tried to ignore every day of her life. "That's why he made sure I'm good with a gun, a horse, and that I'm a fast runner," she said.

"Well, that's mighty fine," he said. "But that don't mean ya shouldn't be afraid." He was getting under her skin now—implying things that did frighten her.

"I told you, I ain't afraid of nothin', and I can take care of myself just fine."

"All righty," the stranger mumbled. "Then take off a-runnin'. I'll give ya a good start and see if I can catch ya."

Cherry was angry, yes—but suddenly her fear was more intense than her anger. She knew the point he was trying to make. Black Jack and his boys had always been up to no good. Yet the fact was most of the young women in town were glad of Pinky Chitter's stubborn and possessive personality. Black Jack wouldn't dare to fiddle with another woman in Blue Water. She suspected Pinky Chitter was the only person Jack was afraid of—afraid she might shoot him square in the back if he strayed too far.

It was then she realized, however—realized

Pinky Chitter didn't have such an acquaintance with the stranger. She guessed the stranger pretty much did as he pleased. Suddenly, she realized she was most likely very fortunate the stranger seemed uninterested in her. Still, she knew she could outrun him. He didn't mean to shoot her—of that she was certain. And if he meant to do anything else—well, there wasn't anybody in Blue Water that could outrun Cherry Ray!

Without another word, Cherry took off like a gunshot. Leaping over a smaller boulder, she headed for the break in the tree line and home.

She was quick, he couldn't deny it. For a moment he wondered if she really might be able to outrun him. Still, he had to get it through her thick little skull—a woman had to be careful in a town like Blue Water, whether or not she was dressed like a boy.

He took out after the girl. He'd give her a little hope—let her stay ahead of him for just a moment or two. But after that—well, the little pup needed to learn a lesson.

Cherry smiled as she ran, dodged a tree stump, and leapt over another. The breeze felt good on her face. She could see the tree line ahead, the pasture beyond. In another minute, she'd break free of the trees, and then he'd see! Once she hit the pasture, she knew no one could catch her then.

"Oof!" Cherry felt the air leave her lungs as strong arms suddenly circled her from behind. Gasping as she felt herself lifted, her feet no longer touched the ground. The breath was knocked from her again when she landed hard on top of the stranger as he clutched her to him and hurled them both to the ground.

"Let me go! Let me go!" she shouted. He'd caught her! How infuriating! Struggling and kicking, she tried to break free, but the stranger was far and away stronger than she was. In a few brief moments, Cherry found herself lying on the ground, hands pinned above her head as the stranger sat on her legs. She felt her bosom rising and falling with the quickened breath of exertion and irritation. Narrowing her eyes, she attempted to glower her fiercest glare at the man.

Using one hand to pin her hands to the ground, the stranger took her chin in his other. "Now you listen here, girl," he said, trying to ignore the way her soft brown hair cascaded over the grass beneath them. In the struggle, her man's hat had fallen from her head, revealing her long, wavy, chestnut hair and allowing the sun to illuminate the tender beauty of her face. "Wearin' boys clothes don't hide ya as good as ya might think . . . and with all that's goin' on 'round these parts, you need to take yer britches down a size or two and be more careful."

His eyes lingered a moment on the inviting pink of the girl's full lips. Dang, she was a pretty thing! It was exactly what worried him. He remembered the first moment he'd seen her the day before—he'd known at once she was a pretty girl trying to hide under a boy's hat and britches. He was certain Black Jack Haley and his boys had noticed it too. He wondered if her daddy knew he'd only drawn attention to his pretty daughter by dressing her up so.

"You only caught me 'cause I let ya," she said, glaring at him with unbridled daring.

He almost laughed out loud. What a green-broke filly the girl was! Hotheaded, overconfident, and asking for trouble. "Now that's a dern lie and ya know it," he told her as she squirmed, attempting to free herself. "Where do you live?"

"I told you," she said, still glaring at him. "This here's my pa's ranch. Our ranch house is just over yonder."

"Then we best get ya home so yer pa can paddle yer hind end a good bit."

Oh, he was arrogant! Who did this stranger think he was—Abe Lincoln? Treating her like a child, throwing her down on the ground. Of course, in the corner of her mind that she was endeavoring to ignore, she knew he was right—he'd caught her far too easily. She guessed she was lucky the stranger hadn't taken any interest in her—didn't find her attractive enough to take advantage of.

"He's liable to paddle yers for treatin' me like this!" she threatened however. She couldn't let him know how completely he'd rattled her.

"Well," he began, "we'll just see who gets paddled when he finds out you were spyin' on me while I was bathin' in the crick."

Standing, he pulled her to her feet, taking hold of the back of her shirt collar. He reached down, picked up her hat, and plopped it on her head.

"Now march, you scrawny little pup," he said, pushing her forward. He still held tightly to the back of her shirt collar. When she tried to bolt and run, he simply pulled her back with a firm grip.

Cherry swallowed hard. Boy oh boy, was her pa gonna be mad! Hadn't he just finished telling her to stay away from the stranger? Moments before the Parker kids had appeared on the front porch—hadn't her pa just warned her about it? Furthermore, hadn't he warned her away from any mischief? And where was she now? Why, in the clutches of the very stranger her pa had warned her to stay away from—awash with mischief!

"Wait, wait, wait," she said, stopping dead in her tracks.

"What?"

Cherry turned too look at him, but he held fast to her shirt. "Why . . . why don't we just call this a draw?" she asked. "Why don't we just say I've learned my lesson? I'm even willin' to admit yer a faster runner than me."

She could swear she saw a twinkle of amusement flash in the stranger's dark eyes, even though his frown persisted.

"I am a faster runner than you, and I hope you have learned yer lesson," the stranger said. "But I still think yer pa needs to know what you been up to." Without another word, he turned her toward the house, forcing her to march in front of him.

It seemed only a matter of moments before she stood on the front porch facing the door of the ranch house.

"Go on, girl," the stranger said. "Let us in."

"Mister . . . I don't think you quite understand who my pa is."

"I don't care if he's the President of the United States," he growled as he reached forward and opened the door.

She stumbled as the stranger forced her into the house. Considering Mrs. Blakely's dramatic gasp and the way in which her eyes widened, her hands going to cover her mouth, Cherry knew she was in trouble. It was only at that moment she realized—the stranger still wore nothing but his boots, britches, and a gun.

CHAPTER THREE

"Arthur!" Mrs. Blakely screamed. "Arthur! Bring yer gun!"

"No, no, no!" Cherry said, shaking her head at Mrs. Blakely. "It's fine. He's fine. He's just—"

"You let that girl go this instant!" Mrs. Blakely shouted at the stranger. "Her pa will drop you cold dead on the floor if ya harmed a hair on her head!"

The stranger raised his free hand, stretching his arm out at his side in a gesture he meant no ill. "Ma'am, I—" the stranger began.

"He'll drop you cold dead!" a now nearly hysterical Mrs. Blakely shouted.

"He didn't do anythin', Mrs. Blakely. Calm yerself down," Cherry said.

Still, she wondered why the stranger had not released his grip on the back of her shirt. Her mind instantly drawn to *Oklahoma Jenny and the Pistoleer*, she wondered if the stranger held fast to her simply for his own protection. Hadn't the pistoleer held onto Oklahoma Jenny until he'd been certain Sheriff Tate wouldn't shoot him? In her soul, she knew the stranger didn't mean to hurt her—for if he had, he'd have already done it.

The stranger remained perfectly still as Lefty

Pierce rounded the corner, pistol drawn. Cherry's pa followed close behind, a crutch under one arm, a rifle aimed low with the other.

"Cherry?" Arthur Ray asked. He wore a threatening frown, but she knew he was concerned—even frightened. She'd never seen her pa frightened, and it worried her.

"It's all right, Pa. He's fine. He just brought me home."

"What're ya doin' with my girl there, boy?" Arthur growled, seeming to ignore Cherry.

"I'm just bringin' yer lost pup home, sir," the stranger said. "Found her down by the crick and was just bringin' her on home."

"Well, she's home, and ya better let her go before ya find a bullet through yer skull, boy," Arthur said.

"It—it ain't his fault, Pa," Cherry stammered as she felt the stranger release her shirt. She glanced back to see him standing with both hands raised, arms outstretched at his sides.

"*Isn't* his fault, Cherry," Mrs. Blakely whispered.

Cherry rolled her eyes, certain Mrs. Blakely would be nagging her from the grave thirty years down the road.

"Well then, he better get to doin' some explainin' 'fore I drop him cold where he stands," Arthur said.

"But, Pa—"

"Hush, Cherry," Arthur interrupted. "Let him get his tongue to waggin' before my finger twitches on this here trigger."

Cherry swallowed hard. An uncomfortable sort of panic was rising in her. What if her pa's finger did twitch? What if her pa shot the handsome stranger before he had a chance to explain it was all her fault? Cherry, normally so calm and brave, frowned when she felt her arms and hands begin to tremble with anxiety. What had she done? Silently, she scolded herself—not for spying on the stranger while he was in the creek but for getting caught.

"My name's Lobo, sir," the stranger said.

"Ain't that nice," Arthur growled, his frown deepening as he glared at the man.

"I come across yer daughter while I was bathin' in the crick, yonder," the stranger continued. "I tried to tell her plain and simple that a girl oughta not be out about such mischief, sir. But she wouldn't hear of it, and I thought I might should bring her on home for her pa to talk with."

"Lobo?" Arthur asked. "Lobo what?"

"Just Lobo."

Cherry watched as her pa looked the stranger over head to toe.

"Ya say ya was bathin'?" Arthur asked.

"Yes, sir," the stranger answered. "I was told it was a fine spot for a man to get his thoughts in a right row. I didn't mean no harm."

"Exactly how did you come across her if you was in the crick?" Arthur asked.

"I heard somethin' . . . a noise close by," the stranger explained.

Cherry shook her head, wondering, for her own sake, why the stranger had to be so dang honest with her pa. "I got out of the crick real quick, grabbed up my britches, boots, and pistol, and found yer daughter hidin' behind a rock."

"Spyin' on a man havin' a bath, Cherry?" Mrs. Blakely gasped. "Mercy sakes, Arthur!"

"I expect she was just curious, ma'am," the stranger said. "I-I mean, bein' that I'm new in town and all," he added when Mrs. Blakely gasped.

Cherry watched as her pa used his crutch to hop forward. She felt guilty when her pa frowned at her and shook his head with disapproval.

"Didn't I just warn you, girl? Didn't I just warn ya about gettin' into mischief?"

"Yes, Pa."

"Seems I'm the one owin' an apology here, Lobo," Arthur said, lowering his rifle and bracing his crutch under his arm as he offered his hand to the stranger.

"Not at all, sir," the stranger said. With a weary glance at Lefty Pierce, the stranger lowered his arms and grasped Arthur's hand with a firm grip. "Thinkin' on it now, it musta been a might shockin' . . . me standin' here only half-dressed with yer daughter in hand. I thank ya for not shootin' before askin' questions, Mr. . . . uh . . . Mr. . . ."

"Arthur Ray. This here's Lefty Pierce and Mrs. Fiona Blakely."

"Howdy, ma'am," the stranger said, nodding to Mrs. Blakely. "Mr. Pierce," he added with a nod in Lefty's direction.

"And I'm guessin' you already know my daughter, Cherry . . . probably better'n you'd like to."

Cherry felt herself blush apple-red as the stranger nodded.

"I'm afraid she knows me better than she probably wanted to too," the stranger said. She could feel his gaze on her—hear the disapproval in his voice. "Arthur Ray?" the stranger suddenly mumbled. "Out—out of San Antonio?"

Cherry looked to the stranger. It seemed he'd paled a bit. She looked to her pa to see his eyes narrow as he nodded.

The stranger nodded and said, "Ain't that a kicker."

"It can be," Arthur said.

Cherry frowned. She was certain something unspoken had passed between her pa and the stranger, but she didn't know what.

"Well, then, I'll be headin' on back to the crick to fetch my shirt and hat," the stranger said.

"That there's a good idea," Arthur said.

The stranger nodded. Cherry felt her brow pucker with bewilderment. She figured the stranger had heard the name of Arthur Ray before—that much was obvious from his reaction and the fact he knew where her pa was from. Yet it was the unspoken things passing between them—a sort of threatening understanding—that was what puzzled her.

"Sorry to have startled ya, ma'am," the stranger said to Mrs. Blakely. "You all have a nice evenin'."

With that, the stranger turned and left by way of the front door. Cherry watched him go—watched the muscles in his arms and back move with the rhythm of his saunter. She suddenly felt disappointed, sad somehow—as if watching him walk away was the worst moment of her life.

"So that's Lobo McCoy," Cherry heard Lefty Pierce mutter.

Cherry turned to see that her pa, Lefty, and Mrs. Blakely stood behind her watching the stranger walk back toward the creek as well.

"Yep," Arthur said. "Lobo McCoy . . . right here in Blue Water."

"You've heard of him?" Cherry asked, irritated she didn't share in the knowledge her pa and Lefty owned. "Who is he?"

"A man you'd do well enough to stay far away from, Cherry," Arthur said. Her pa reached out and gripped her shoulder while still leaning on his crutch. "You stay out of that man's way, Cherry," he said. "Do you hear me? I mean it! You stay away from that man."

"Why? Who is he?"

"He's Lobo McCoy," Lefty answered, his voice hushed with obvious awe.

"And don't go tellin' nobody who he is, Cherry," Arthur said. "Look me in the eye and promise me you won't tell nobody his full name. He done told us his name was Lobo, so I 'spect he plans on tellin' folks that much. But don't you go speakin' a word of McCoy to nobody! You hear me?"

"Well, yes, Pa, but—"

"I mean it this time, Cherry," Arthur said.

Cherry had never seen her pa so severe—never seen such fear in his eyes. "What's he done, pa?" she asked in a whisper.

"Never you mind that. You just stay out of his way and let him be about his business in Blue Water. Promise me, Cherry. You stand here and promise me ya won't go causin' that man any more trouble."

"Is he that dangerous, Pa?" Her curiosity was too alive to ignore. Yet to imagine the handsome stranger as being so bad an outlaw that her pa would worry so severely—she didn't want to believe it! "What's he done?"

"Danger rode into Blue Water the moment that man did, Cherry," Arthur began, "and I don't want you in the middle of it. Promise me."

"All right, Pa," Cherry mumbled halfheartedly.

"Cherry!" he scolded.

"All right!"

Still, as she watched Lobo McCoy rake his fingers through his dark, wet hair as he headed for the creek, Cherry knew she would never be able to keep her promise to her pa. Not once—not once in the whole of her life had a man like Lobo McCoy crossed her path. Handsome, powerful, fearless, yet cautious too, Lobo McCoy marked the standard of what every man should be in Cherry's mind. She smiled as she thought of Oklahoma Jenny and Sheriff Tate. It seemed to her that Sheriff Tate was such a man as Lobo McCoy. Less exciting—calmer perhaps—but suddenly, she could see why Oklahoma Jenny loved Sheriff Tate so thoroughly. Something about Sheriff Tate attracted and held onto Jenny's soul, and Cherry knew in that moment that Lobo McCoy held onto hers. She had no intention of keeping away from him—danger or no danger.

"Get on in and close that door," Mrs. Blakely said.

Cherry could hear the muffled tap of her pa's crutch. He and Lefty were heading for the parlor.

"Come on, Cherry," her pa said. "I want to know how you came to be peekin' on that man while he was bathin'. And what happened to them Parker boys? Wasn't they with ya when ya left the house?"

"I'm comin'," Cherry said. Yet she lingered a moment more—watching as the stranger met the tree line and disappeared from her sight.

"Yep," she whispered to herself. "I don't know how I'm gonna do it . . . but I want you for my own, Lobo McCoy." She smiled as she closed the door. "And when I set my mind to somethin', nothin' can stop me. Not even Pa."

Sunday morning dawned bright and hopeful for Cherry Ray. Sitting beside her pa in the buggy, she wondered if the Parker children would be at church. As Mrs. Blakely prattled on from the backseat of the buggy, Cherry's thoughts lingered on Lobo McCoy—just as they had nearly every moment for the past three days. Would he be at church? she wondered. Surely not. Not that he didn't seem the type—it was just—well, something else.

For three days, Cherry had wondered about her pa's reaction when Lobo had asked if he was from San Antonio. For three days, she'd thought of the way Lobo had not attempted to force any sort of unwanted attention on her when he'd found her spying on him while he bathed. Well, sure—knowing who her pa was, Black Jack wouldn't have touched her either. Still, Lobo hadn't known who her pa was when he'd first found her behind the rock. Yet he hadn't harmed her, and she was certain he wasn't an outlaw. At least not the sort Black Jack Haley was.

Thus, Cherry's mind had been concocting all sorts of possibilities concerning the handsome stranger, Lobo McCoy. Perhaps he wasn't any sort of bad man at all—simply someone stopping over in Blue Water on his way to somewhere else. Maybe he had kin in Mexico and was traveling on to visit them. His pants certainly were a testament to his having been there at some point in his life.

Yet try as she might to justify his mysterious behavior, Cherry knew her pa knew something she didn't. The fact that he wouldn't give her any more details on what he did know about Lobo McCoy nagged at her worse than ever Fiona Blakely did. Her pa saw danger in Lobo's wake. Cherry knew this simple fact meant she should see danger too—but she couldn't. How could danger look so delicious dressed in nothing but boots and britches?

"And don't whip yer fan back and forth so fast, Cherry. It draws attention and makes the preacher think yer not interested in his sermon," Mrs. Blakely was saying.

"I won't," Cherry said, releasing an exasperated sigh.

"You will," Mrs. Blakely said. "You always do."

"You look mighty purty in that there pink dress, Cherry," Arthur said.

Cherry looked to him and smiled. She knew he was only trying to soften Mrs. Blakely's eternal nagging. Still, she was certain that, in her pa's eyes, she did look pretty.

"Thanks, Pa," she said, wrapping her arms around one of his still strong ones and laying her head on his shoulder.

"And I don't know if ya need to be a runnin' off with those Parker children after services today," Mrs. Blakely said. "You always come home dustier than any trail hand at the ranch."

"I like the Parker children. They're—they're interesting. And besides, I'm always home in time for Sunday supper."

"Well, yer old enough ya oughta be cookin' Sunday supper by now," Mrs. Blakely said.

"How 'bout we just ride the rest of the way into town in quiet contemplation of the Lord's day," Arthur said.

"Of course, Pa," Cherry said, stifling a giggle. She could tell by the way her pa rolled his eyes that he too was tired of Mrs. Blakely's perpetual nagging.

It was a glorious day! The grasses and wildflowers were especially fragrant, and the birds flittered hither and yon as if not a care in the world owned them.

Cherry's thoughts immediately returned to Lobo McCoy. She'd stayed up far too late the night before reading *Oklahoma Jenny and the*

Pistoleer. Over and over she'd read her favorite pages—the pages where Sheriff Tate saved Oklahoma Jenny from certain death at the hands of the pistoleer, then brazenly kissed her in front of all the townsfolk. It was one of her favorite parts of any of her Oklahoma Jenny books. Closing her eyes, she could just imagine it—see it in her mind's eye, just as the scandalous book described it. She could see Oklahoma Jenny wrapped tight in Sheriff Tate's strong arms—their lips pressed together in a kiss! The thought of it always caused her to sigh, and today was no different.

"I know how ya feel, Cherry," Arthur said.

"What's that, Pa?" she asked, opening her eyes once more.

"It *is* a beautiful day."

Cherry realized he'd misunderstood the reason for her sigh. Smiling, she nodded at him and kissed him sweetly on the cheek.

She hoped Lobo McCoy was in town even if he wasn't in church. She hoped he would be somewhere near when they drove in and would see her dressed as a woman instead of a man. Oh, how she loathed dressing in men's clothes! It was rare that she let herself admit the fact, but every Sunday the realization was put to her again. Every Sunday as she put on a soft pastel-colored dress and stood before the mirror in her room, she grew angry—angry at having to dress in men's clothes to save her pa worry. Every Sunday when she studied her reflection, pleased with having been able to pull her hair up, a few soft curls cascading over her neck and shoulders—every Sunday frustration grew thick in her veins. Still, her pa was her pa, and he loved her—this she knew for certain. He cared for her, worried for her, and only meant to keep her safe. And so, she endured it—waiting for the day when Black Jack Haley would leave Blue Water for good and she could dress as femininely as she liked every day of her life.

The service had been enjoyable enough. The preacher had spoken of "goodwill toward men," and it had put Cherry's mind to thinking on Christmas. She always enjoyed thinking on Christmas, and she left the small white church with a smile on her face and a lighthearted sensation in her bosom.

"Cherry," Billy Parker said as he rather trotted down the church steps behind her. "We're goin' for our Sunday walk. Do ya wanna come with us?"

"Sure."

She ignored Mrs. Blakely's heavy sigh and the way the elderly woman rolled her eyes with obvious disapproval.

Instead, she asked her pa, "Is it all right if I go, Pa? It's just a Sunday walk."

Cherry watched as her pa's eyes narrowed.

"Last time you was out with these Parker boys,

ya got yerself drug home by the scruff of the neck," he reminded.

"It's just a Sunday walk, Pa."

Arthur Ray sighed. What could he do? He worried about Cherry—worried about the fact she'd rather run headlong into mischief with a bunch of kids than spend time with the other young ladies in town closer to her own age. Still, it was nobody's fault but his. He was the one who insisted she dress like a boy in order to keep the likes of Black Jack Haley from eyeing her up. Yet he wondered if he'd damaged her in another way—by not letting her be the young lady she so obviously was. Furthermore, he hadn't liked the way her eyes had been so lit up and full of fire the day Lobo McCoy had drug her on back to the ranch house. Lobo had rattled Cherry—Arthur knew it all too well by the color in her cheeks and the twinkle in her eyes the day the man had showed up at the house, Cherry Ray in hand.

Arthur looked down the street to where the other young ladies of Blue Water were walking arm in arm with their beaus or potential beaus. He looked back at Cherry, waiting expectantly and quite obviously impatiently, to run off with Billy Parker. She ought to be linked on the arm of some cowboy, on her way to marriage and starting a family of her own.

Still, how could he refuse her? The pure excitement lighting her eyes could not be denied. Cherry liked spending time with the Parker kids. And besides, Arthur hadn't seen hide nor hair of Lobo McCoy all day. Chances were he wasn't anywhere near to town—nowhere near to catch Cherry's attention.

"Oh, go on then," Arthur said. "But be home by supper, Cherry."

"I will, Pa," she said, quickly kissing him on the cheek.

"Come on, Cherry," Billy said, taking hold of her hand and tugging her in the direction Pocket and Laura were already running. "There's a dead prairie dog a-rottin' just behind the church here. It's just crawlin' with maggots. You just gotta see it!"

Cherry giggled and followed as Billy led her to a prairie dog mound near the church.

"Arthur Ray!" Fiona began scolding almost instantly. "You've got to keep the reins tighter on that girl!"

"Oh, some feller will come along and marry her soon enough, Fiona," he said. "Then the reins will be pulled tight enough, I'm afraid."

"No feller's gonna want her if she doesn't start acting more like a lady. You've either gotta let her be a woman, Arthur . . . or move her somewhere where she can be one."

"I know," Arthur mumbled. "I know."

Arthur watched his daughter lift her skirt and

begin running after the Parker children. She was so beautiful. So beautiful! Especially on Sundays. Arthur never missed the way the cowboys and other men in town always eyed Cherry in church every Sunday. If it hadn't been for Fiona's infernal nagging on the need for respecting the Lord on the Sabbath, Arthur would've kept Cherry hidden in men's clothes all seven days of the week. Yet in his heart he knew he was wrong to stifle Cherry's need to be feminine and pretty.

He shook his head as the vision of Lobo McCoy dripping wet and only half-dressed came to his mind again. How could Cherry have avoided being overcome by such a man? Especially when her pa's insistence to stay hidden left her the likes of only young Billy Parker to give her any masculine attention.

Breathing a heavy sigh, Arthur helped Fiona into the buggy before tossing his crutches in and lifting himself into the seat. Glancing around once more, relieved that Lobo McCoy seemed to be nowhere in sight, Arthur mumbled, "Gid-up," and slapped the lines at the back of the horse.

With one final glance in Cherry's direction, he smiled and chuckled when he saw her and the three Parker children leaning over as they studied something on the ground. What mischief could there be linked to a dead prairie dog? None. He'd let her have her Sunday walk with the Parkers and try not to think about Lobo McCoy and the reason he'd come to Blue Water.

"I bet there's a bucketful of 'em," Laura said, wrinkling her nose as she gazed down at the maggots writhing in the open and rotting stomach of the dead prairie dog.

"That wouldn't fill no bucket," Pocket argued. "But there's a good handful or two."

"Looks like somebody shot it," Billy said. "Don't ya think, Cherry?"

"Yeah," she said, frowning. "And right through the head."

"Good shootin', whoever it was," Billy said.

"Black Jack ain't back in town, is he?" Cherry asked.

Black Jack liked to shoot prairie dogs. He used them for practicing his draw. Oh, Cherry and her pa shot plenty of prairie dogs too. Prairie dog burrows were heck on cattle; she couldn't even count the number of cows her pa had had to put down due to a broken leg from stepping in a prairie dog burrow. Still, she began to feel an odd sense of discomfort washing over her. It was Sunday, and she wasn't dressed like a man. The last time Black Jack had seen her dressed like the woman that she was—well, she still hadn't told her pa about that incident. And she didn't plan to!

"Nope," Pocket said. "And we'd know if he

was. Our pa keeps out of town when Jack's here . . . even on Sundays."

"Good," Cherry said, feeling somewhat relieved.

"Billy? Pocket? Laura Parker! Where have you children run off to now?"

It was Mrs. Parker. Cherry straightened, shading her eyes from the sun with one hand as she looked in the direction of the church. Mrs. Parker stood in front of the church hollering like there was no tomorrow.

"We're over here, Mama!" Laura called.

Mrs. Parker turned around. Upon seeing the children, she placed a fist on each hip and shouted, "You children get on home! We've got company comin' for supper, and I need help." Raising one hand to wave, she added, "Hey there, Cherry! How's yer pa?"

"Just fine, Mrs. Parker. Thank you," she said waving in return.

"I'm sorry the children can't play longer today, Cherry," Mrs. Parker called. "I've got company and need them home."

"That's fine, Mrs. Parker. You have a nice day." She waved again, feeling ridiculous about the fact that Mrs. Parker would have to explain to a nineteen-year-old woman why her children couldn't stay and play.

"Sorry, Cherry," Billy said. "I guess we better go."

"That's fine," she said, forcing a smile. "I'll see you all tomorrow or the next day."

"Bye-bye, Cherry," Laura said as she ran off to meet her mother.

"Maybe if ya turn it over, you'll find some more maggots underneath," Pocket said as he followed his sister.

"I wish I was older, Cherry Ray," Billy said, kicking a nearby dirt mound. "Then Ma couldn't tell me what to do . . . and I could go sparkin' with you once in a while."

Cherry's mouth dropped open in astonished delight. How sweet! "That's the sweetest thing anybody has said to me in as long as I can remember, Billy! Thank you."

"Well," Billy began, "you just be sure that when you do get a feller . . . you just be sure he's got some fun in him, Cherry. You couldn't live without fun. I may be too young fer ya . . . but I know ya purty well, and you need to have fun."

"I do at that, Billy Parker. Thanks for showin' me this," she said, pointing to the maggoty prairie dog. "And thanks for lettin' me keep Ol' Red. You found him, and I'm sure you would've liked to have taken him to yer house."

"Billy Parker!" Mrs. Parker hollered.

"Ma woulda never let me drag that old dried-up wolf home. Besides, you'll take better care of him than I would've. See ya tomorrow, Cherry."

"All right," Cherry giggled as the boy rather unwillingly swaggered after his siblings.

What a sweet boy Billy Parker was! Cherry had often wondered, were Billy older or were she younger, would they have been sweethearts in some regard? Still, he was much younger, and she saw him only as a sweet little friend. It did make her feel delighted, however—the fact that he wished he were older for her sake.

Cherry glanced down at the maggoty prairie dog. Releasing a heavy sigh, she turned and began walking toward town. She'd stay behind the buildings, out of sight if she could. Still, she couldn't resist going into town and hoping to catch a glimpse of Lobo McCoy. She wished she'd snuck an Oklahoma Jenny book to church with her. She could've found a quiet spot and enjoyed a chapter or two if her search for Lobo proved unsuccessful.

As Cherry drew nearer to town, she could hear the music of the piano from the saloon carried on the breeze. She smiled, knowing full well Mrs. Fiona Blakely would have a loco fit if she knew Cherry was lurking behind the general store, peering across the street into the open saloon doors on a Sunday!

Cherry could hear Pinky Chitter singing. She could hear the laughter and applause of the men gambling in the saloon as Pinky ended one song and began another. Still, she couldn't quite see into the saloon, and she was suddenly overcome with curiosity. Was Lobo McCoy inside? She felt sickened at the thought. Surely a man who would march a girl home from a creek without taking advantage of her wouldn't be loitering in a saloon. Yet most men in town stopped by the saloon once in a while—whether for a game of cards, a smelly old drink, or a visit with Pinky or one of her girls.

Cherry felt angry, overly warm at the thought of Lobo McCoy being in the saloon—for any reason. She had to know if he were in there at that moment. She had to! Carefully, she slipped into the open space between the general store and the blacksmith's building. Several old barrels, some on their sides and some sitting straight up, had been placed in the alley, and Cherry ducked down behind one of them.

Straining her eyes, she peered across the street into the saloon. She could see Pinky sitting on top of the piano as Petey Smith played. She could see several men at a table playing cards, but she couldn't be certain if any of them were Lobo McCoy.

"He's trouble. It's plain obvious."

Two men were coming out of the blacksmith's building—Remmy Cooper and the blacksmith, Mr. Murphy. It was Mr. Murphy who was speaking, and his next words caused Cherry's eyebrows to raise with curiosity.

"Says his name's Lobo but won't say no more."

"Maybe he's just passin' through," Remmy offered.

"Oh, I'm sure he is . . . passin' through to join ol' Jack and his boys."

They were coming closer! Quickly, Cherry looked around. A nearby barrel on its side looked big enough! Feetfirst, she squeezed into the barrel. Remmy and Mr. Murphy would stop their conversation about Lobo McCoy dead cold if they saw her—and she wanted to hear more.

"He looks like a nice enough feller," Remmy said. "He ain't caused no trouble yet."

"That's 'cause he's waitin' . . . waitin' for Jack to get back from hidin' out after that mess in San Antone."

"Afternoon, gentlemen."

Cherry clamped her hand tight over her mouth, startled by the sound of his voice. Daring to look out of the top of the barrel, she gasped again as she saw another set of legs join those of Remmy Cooper and Mr. Murphy. All three men stepped back several steps, and Cherry saw two skirts walk by.

"Howdy," Remmy said as the skirts swished past them.

Lobo McCoy was so close, Cherry could've reached and pulled one of the silver buttons off his vaquero's pants. She tried to remain calm—

tried to breathe normally. Yet his sudden and unexpected nearness had caused her heart to begin hammering so brutally within her bosom she was certain the men would hear it!

"Hey there, Lobo," Mr. Murphy greeted. "What can I do fer ya?"

Cherry wrinkled her nose, irritated with the man's hypocrisy.

"My horse threw a shoe," Lobo said. "I was wonderin' if ya had the time to shoe him up. I tied him up just over there. I know it's Sunday, but I wouldn't ask it of ya if it weren't important. I want him kept up in case I need to ride out for some reason."

The sound of his voice washed over Cherry like a refreshing summer rain. And yet—what had he said? He wanted his horse ready in case he needed to ride out for some reason? What kind of a man couldn't wait one day to have his horse shod?

"I'll pay ya handsomely," Lobo added, "for the inconvenience of it bein' Sunday and all."

"You got a deal, Lobo," Mr. Murphy said. "I'll get to it now."

Cherry watched as Mr. Murphy headed back toward his shop, his legs disappearing from her view.

"Name's Remmy Cooper."

"Lobo."

"Nice to meet ya," Remmy said. "Hope to get

to know ya better, but for now I gotta be headin' on back to the ranch."

"Arthur Ray's place?"

Remmy chuckled. "Nope. I weren't lucky enough to get on with Arthur last fall. I run cattle for ol' John Brooks. You have a good day."

"Same to you."

Cherry watched as Remmy Cooper's legs disappeared too. She tried to calm the increased beating of her heart and breath as she studied Lobo McCoy's legs. His boots were worn and dusty, but the silver buttons on the legs of his britches looked as polished as a new silver dollar. She wondered if they were real silver—surely not. Yet, as close as she was to them, she was nearly certain they were. It took every ounce of self-control she could muster not to reach out and touch one of the buttons.

He moved—walked two steps until he was at the side of the barrel instead of at the top. Cherry gasped as she heard his boot hit the side of the barrel—braced her arms against the inside curves of the barrel as Lobo McCoy began to rock the barrel back and forth using his foot. He knew! He had to know someone was in the barrel. But how? She'd been so still, so very quiet.

Cherry began to tremble as Lobo's face suddenly appeared at the barrel's top opening. He breathed a sigh and scowled at her. "Cherry Ray . . . what in tarnation are ya up to now?"

CHAPTER FOUR

Panic leapt to Cherry's bosom as she gazed into the dark, alluring eyes of Lobo McCoy. Hunkering down in front of the barrel, he shook his head. He removed his hat, ran his fingers through his hair, and replaced it before looking at her again.

"You were spyin' on them men, weren't ya?" he asked.

She shook her head, horrified at being caught spying once more.

"I . . . I was out for a Sunday walk and—" she stammered.

"You were out for a Sunday walk . . . in an old empty barrel?"

"Oh, please don't drag me back to my pa!" she begged. She was suddenly more afraid of another reprimand at her pa's hand than she was of further humiliation at Lobo's. "He'll skin me alive if he finds out I got caught again."

She watched as Lobo shook his head. He looked around as if making certain no one else was watching them.

"Here," he said. He stood, and Cherry tried to ignore the hot blush of embarrassment rising to her cheeks. She felt the barrel being righted and looked up into the sky a moment before Lobo's handsome face appeared above her.

"Stand up, and I'll haul ya on outta there," he said.

"Is anybody lookin'?"

"Nope."

She reached up, taking hold of the lip of the barrel on either side. Pulling herself up, she stood. She glanced away, entirely humiliated when Lobo sighed and shook his head.

"Please don't tell my pa about this," she begged in a whisper. "He worries too awful much about me already."

"Seems to me he has good reason," Lobo mumbled as he reached out, taking her waist between strong hands and lifting her out of the barrel.

"Please, mister," she pleaded. "I won't be any more trouble to you—I swear it! Just don't march me home again and tell my pa."

Unexpectedly, a swarm of butterflies erupted in Cherry's stomach at the sight of Lobo McCoy's sudden laughter and stunning smile. His entire countenance had changed, and he was only all the more unsettlingly handsome!

"I suppose I can keep from tellin' yer pa," he said, shaking his head with obvious amusement. "But I do think I oughta make sure ya get home," he said, taking hold of her arm as if he were scolding a child. "Hard tellin' how much more trouble ya might step in between here and there."

"I-I can find my way fine by myself." The truth

was she wanted nothing more in all the world than for Lobo McCoy to take her home. Just to be in his company would be worth any discipline her pa might dish out. Still, she had to make him think she didn't want his company. Didn't she?

"My horse threw a shoe this mornin', so we'll hafta walk," he said. He paused, smiling as he looked at her. "Of course, you already knew that, didn't ya?"

Cherry blushed the very color of her name. How humiliating! What must he think of her? She scolded herself for thinking even for one moment that she might be able to capture the attention of the likes of Lobo McCoy. Her—with her ridiculous behavior and even more ridiculous clothing! It was only then she remembered—she wasn't dressed in any ridiculous fashion that day. It was Sunday, and she was dressed like a lady! She wondered if this was the reason he held tight to her arm instead of to the back collar of her dress.

"How did ya end up in that barrel?" he asked.

"I crawled in." Cherry had always possessed a thicker streak of smart aleck than did most women her age, and when Lobo chuckled, she guessed it wasn't wasted on him.

"I saw that much," he said. "That's how I knew you were in there. I mean, why ain't you in church or somethin'? Ya look dressed for more than hidin' in barrels and spyin' on men."

"I was in church. It let out, and Billy Parker said there was a dead, maggoty prairie dog out behind the church house, and I wanted to see it."

"I shot that prairie dog the other mornin'. But that still don't explain how you ended up in a barrel."

"You shot it? For a minute, we wondered if Black Jack was back in town . . . 'cause he's the only one in Blue Water who can dead-eye a prairie dog like that. Him and my pa . . . and me, of course." Would it work? Would Lobo be distracted enough with the talk about Black Jack to forget about why or why not she had crawled into the barrel?

"You?" he asked. "You can shoot a prairie dog at a run for his burrow?"

"I sure can."

"From where? Sittin' on top of the burrow?"

Cherry looked at him and glared. "From a greater distance than most anybody. Me and Pa used to sit out on the back porch and pick 'em off when I was growin' up. The little devils are heck on a herd of cattle, ya know."

"So I've been told," he said.

Cherry thrilled through and through as he tightened his grip on her arm a little.

"You think I'm joshin' with ya. You don't believe I'm as good a shot as you."

"Yer sure good at shootin' off yer mouth, that's for dang sure," he said.

"I'll prove it to ya," Cherry said. "Give me yer gun, and I'll prove it."

"Darlin', I ain't gonna give ya nothin' that might get ya in more trouble than ya already manage to get into yerself."

"Yer afraid I'm a better shot than you," Cherry said, stopping and yanking her arm from his grasp.

"I ain't afraid of nothin'," Lobo said. "And you ain't a better shot than me."

"Then prove it, stranger."

Lobo felt his eyebrows draw together in a frown. This girl was getting under his skin. The banter she had started in trying to distract him from the fact he'd found her hiding in a barrel and eavesdropping on a conversation . . . had actually worked! Furthermore, she'd somehow pushed him into verbally revealing his skills with a gun.

He studied her for a moment—head-to-toe studied her, more than pleased with what he saw. She looked so different all gussied up in a pretty dress, hair softly piled high on her head. Not that she wasn't pretty dressed up like a boy—but she was more akin to "cute" the first two times he'd seen her—as compared with now, when everything masculine in him was drawn to the mischievous twinkle in her eyes, the soft pink of her lips, and the perfect curves of her body.

"I told ya the other day . . . ya ought not to be

flirtin' with the likes of outlaws and gunmen," he said. "You might find yerself in a pickle ya can't get out of."

"And I told ya I ain't flirtin'. If I was . . . you'd know it."

"Is that so?" he asked, entirely intrigued by her confidence.

"It is. And besides . . . I am a better shot than you are." The confidence of her expression lessened a little, and she added, "Or at least as good."

Black Jack wasn't back in town, his horse was getting shod—what else did he have to do on a Sunday afternoon?

Cherry's heart was pounding like Mr. Murphy's hammer on an anvil! Just being near him, in his presence—it was the most invigorating experience of her life. Oh, what she wouldn't give to spend Sunday afternoon with him! She thought of the Saturday evenings Oklahoma Jenny and Sheriff Tate would spend together—shooting old whiskey bottles off fence posts. Of course, Jenny was a better shot than Sheriff Tate, and Cherry doubted she could outshoot Lobo McCoy. Still, she'd give it a try—if only he'd agree.

When Lobo told Cherry to stay put behind the church while he went back to town to pick up some old bottles from the saloon, she was near certain he wouldn't return. But he did! Half an hour later, she watched as Lobo McCoy set the last whiskey bottle on the last fence post. She stood watching him as he sauntered back toward her, having placed one bottle on each of the six fence posts in front of them. Cherry wasn't as accurate with a pistol as she was with a rifle, but she really was a better shot than anyone else in Blue Water—save her pa and Black Jack. She'd even beaten old Lefty Pierce every time he'd challenged her.

"All righty then, Cherry Ray," he said, drawing his pistol from its holster at his hip and handing it to her, butt first. "Let's see how good ya are. I'll even offer to give ya a nickel for each bottle ya hit."

Cherry smiled at him. "I don't need yer money, mister. Showin' you I'm as good as I said I was is all the motivatin' I need."

He chuckled, and the sound sent goose bumps rippling over her arms.

"There ya go then," he said, nodding toward the first bottle.

Cherry took a deep breath. She knew his presence would distract her and might cause her hand to be unsteady. Still, she was determined to get Lobo McCoy's attention—one way or the other. Maybe she didn't have the charm and beauty of some of the girls in town—but she was a better shot.

Taking the pistol in both hands, she took her aim. She was careful at first, making certain her hands were steady and her aim true. Squeezing the trigger of the Colt belonging to Lobo McCoy, she smiled when she saw the whiskey bottle shatter from the fence post.

"Nice!" he chuckled as Cherry took her second aim.

The sound of the pistol shot, and the second whiskey bottle shattering drew another awed response from Lobo. Cherry smiled and shot the third bottle from the next post. Moments later, she smiled as Lobo pulled six more bullets from his gun belt, took the weapon from her, and reloaded it.

"How accurate are you from farther back?" he asked.

"As accurate as anybody." Already they were farther from the fence posts than she was most comfortable with—but she didn't want him to know it.

She smiled, watching him saunter back toward the posts to set up more bottles. A pang pinched deep in her chest—as if something were being slowly driven into her heart as she watched him. He was so much more the man of her very dreams than any man she had ever before met! She thought of Oklahoma Jenny's sister, Pearl— of the time Pearl lost her egg and milk money to a handsome drifter, all for the sake of one kiss.

Cherry wondered what she would be willing to give up for one kiss from Lobo McCoy. She didn't have much—a silver locket that had been her mother's and her Oklahoma Jennys. She doubted Lobo McCoy would find either one of her most cherished possessions worth kissing her for.

"Okey dokee," he said upon his return. "Let's move back."

Taking hold of her arm, he led her back farther and farther until Cherry's nerves and confidence were both a little rattled.

"It's pretty far back," she said as she looked at the bottles sitting on top of the fence posts off in the distance.

"We can move closer." He smiled then, his eyes narrowing as he looked at her. "Or are ya just tryin' to set me up to be the fool?"

Cherry shrugged, forced a confident smile, and held out her hand.

Lobo's eyebrows raised in daring as he handed her the pistol. "If you can get 'em all again, I really will give ya a nickel each," he said.

Cherry swallowed hard. The bottles were far off—just small specks on the horizon—and she was best with a rifle, not a pistol. Still, Lobo's pistol was a good weapon—and accurate. She drew in a deep breath and took aim.

Six shattered whiskey bottles later, Lobo McCoy whistled! Shaking his head, he smiled with approval and clapped his hands several times.

"You've made a believer outta me, Cherry Ray," he said as she handed his gun to him. "You're a mighty fine shot. A mighty fine shot at that!"

Cherry smiled. Surely her shooting skills had captured his attention. She smoothed the skirt of her dress and tried not to blush too boldly with delight.

"I'm much better with a rifle," she said.

"You're surprisin' enough with a pistol, girl," he said, chuckling as he reloaded the gun. "Ever draw from a belt and holster before?"

Cherry shook her head and said, "No. Pa never would let me."

"Well, let's give it a try."

Cherry giggled as she watched Lobo unfasten his gun belt.

"Here now," he said as he reached around her with the gun belt and began fastening it at her waist. He frowned for a moment as he took hold of the two thin leather ties at the tip of the holster. "Hmm. Maybe we shoulda done this the other day when you were wearin' yer britches."

But Cherry was too delighted to let such a simple thing as attire interfere with her stolen moments with Lobo McCoy. "Oh, it'll be fine," she said, slapping his hand gently and stunning him into dropping the leather ties.

Quickly, she hitched up the side of her dress and tied the straps at the back of her knee. She was wearing Lobo McCoy's gun belt! What better thing in the world could there be?

Looking back to him, she felt just a little self-conscious when she saw the high arch of his brows as he looked at the exposed, yet stockinged, calf of her leg.

"Now," she said, drawing his attention back to her face. For a moment, she was near certain his face was a little redder than it had been a moment before. "Show me what to do."

"Um . . . um . . ." he stammered looking from her face to her leg and back. "Just . . . just draw and fire. Best use just one hand, though. In fact, let's move ya a bit closer." He reached out and took hold of her arm, walking her toward the fence posts once more. He hurried over to the first fence post. Picking up one of the few remaining bottles lying on the ground, he set it on top of the post and hurried back.

"Now . . . ya just . . . draw and fire. Keep yer hand relaxed but ready," he said, taking her hand and pressing it against the holster at her thigh. "Slide yer hand up, grab the butt, and trigger on yer way . . . draw and fire."

"It's harder than it looks," she said, glancing down at the gun.

"Don't look down," he instructed, pushing her chin up with one hand. "Keep yer eye on the target, and feel the gun instead of looking at it. And go slow at first—it ain't like someone's steppin' out in the street to gun ya down. It's just a bottle."

Cherry swallowed. He liked the fact she was a good shot—she could tell he really liked that fact—and she didn't want to disappoint him now. Still, she'd never drawn a gun from a holster, and she wasn't good with a pistol using only one hand.

"Go on," he urged. "Go on and give it a try."

"All right." Taking a deep breath, she looked at the whiskey bottle sitting on the fence post. Sliding her hand up and over the holster, she grasped the butt and trigger firmly, drew the gun, and fired. Disappointment nearly drowned her as she saw the chip of wood fly off the fence post below the bottle. She'd missed. Lobo's whistle drew her attention to him, however, and she grinned when she saw him smiling.

"Excellent!" he said, smiling at her. "Try it again. Slow and easy. It'll come to you."

It took four more attempts and Lobo moving her closer to the target, but with the fifth bullet out of the pistol, Cherry hit the bottle.

"I thought you were just tellin' tales when you said you could outshoot me, girl," he said as she handed his gun belt back to him. She watched as he quickly strapped it on and secured the leather ties at his thigh. "But ya weren't, were ya?"

"Nope," Cherry said, smiling at him.

She thought of the first moment she'd seen him—riding in so serious and menacing—intimidating everyone in town with such an intimidating air about him. She'd never imagined he could be any more handsome than he had been in that first moment. She'd never imagined he could be any more handsome than he'd been the day he'd marched her home without his shirt or hat on—but he could be! His easy manner with her now—it sent her entire body to tingling, her mouth to watering for some reason.

He shook his head as he reloaded his pistol and slid it into the holster.

"But what about you?" she asked then. "Who's the better shot out of the two of us?"

Lobo chuckled. "Probably you."

"Were ya sittin' a horse when ya shot that prairie dog?" she asked.

"Of course," he said, as if the circumstance were unimportant.

"And where were ya when ya shot it?"

Lobo shrugged. "I don't know . . . behind the general store, I guess."

Cherry smiled. He was so completely distracted by her shooting skills that he didn't even realize what he'd just revealed to her. To hit a prairie dog dead in the head while in the saddle and all the way back at the general store? It was incredible.

"Come on," he said, as he sauntered back to the posts. "One more round."

"But we're out of bottles."

"Yer good enough," he said as he hunkered down in front of the first post. "We'll just use what's left. See here?" He picked up several bottlenecks—the remains of the whiskey bottles Cherry had already hit. "We'll just use these."

Cherry giggled, shook her head with disbelief at his attention being so drawn to her shot. She watched as he flipped the bottlenecks upside down, balancing them on the smooth, unbroken lips of their tops.

He was chuckling as he hurried back toward her. Drawing his gun, he held it out to her. "Go on," he said. "See what ya can do with those."

"You go," Cherry said however. "You ain't shot one bullet. How do I know ya weren't just talkin' big about yer own skill with a gun?"

As a rule, outlaws were good shooters—gunmen with lethal aim. Although her heart assured her Lobo McCoy was no outlaw, her eyes doubted the fact. If he'd really dropped the prairie dog from the distance he'd said, then Lobo McCoy was as deadly with a pistol as any outlaw she had ever heard of.

"Oh, I—I ain't—I ain't that accurate," he stammered. "My shootin' goes more toward fast than exact."

"Then show me," Cherry said.

Lobo shook his head. "It ain't important," he mumbled.

He was lessening the quality of his skills, she was certain. But why? Furthermore, she had to know—she had to know, once and for all—how good was Lobo McCoy with the pistol at his hip?

"If ya show me . . . I'll tell ya why I was in the barrel in town today."

He smiled and seemed to study the bottlenecks on the fence posts. "I know why ya were in the barrel today. You was listenin' in to what them men were sayin'. Ya probably have yer eye set on that Remmy Cooper feller. I hear he's considered a right handsome man."

It wasn't going to work. Oh, he was dead wrong about the Remmy Cooper part—who would ever look at Remmy Cooper once they'd laid eyes on Lobo McCoy? Still, he was right about the eavesdropping. Though he didn't know what had attracted her to the conversation between Remmy and Mr. Murphy in the first place—the subject being Lobo himself.

"All right then," she said, smiling as an idea began to form in her mind. "If ya show me how fast ya are . . . I promise to tell ya what else I saw while you were bathin' in the crick the other day."

That was it! Lobo McCoy looked up—looked at her with a frown that spoke of unquenchable curiosity.

"Deal," he said. An instant later, he drew, shattering all six bottlenecks from the fence posts before Cherry had even finished gasping!

She knew it then—Cherry knew her heart was attaching itself to a gunman! Lobo had drawn his gun with such lightning speed that she hadn't even realized he'd done so before two shots were already off! He triggered with his right hand, hammering with his left—the fastest shooter Cherry had ever seen.

"What else did ya see?" he asked.

"Wh-what?" Cherry stammered, still stunned by Lobo's speed and accuracy.

"What else did ya see when you was spyin' on me at the crick?" he repeated. His brow was deeply furrowed with a frown—any hint of the smile he'd worn only moments before completely vanished.

"N-nothin'," she admitted. "I . . . I was just tryin' to draw ya out."

Lobo breathed a quick sigh. He shook his head as he reloaded his gun and looked at her once more as he holstered it. "You gotta quit this, girl," he said. "Do ya understand? Hell, yer gonna put yer pa in the grave over worrying about you." Taking hold of her arm, he turned her toward the ranch and began marching her home once more.

Cherry's heart was beating wildly—with both excitement at Lobo's touch and disappointment at having turned his admiration to near instant frustration.

"I was in the barrel because I was tryin' to see into the saloon . . . to see if you were takin' up with Pinky Chitter," Cherry blurted.

Lobo instantly stopped their march and turned her to look at him. "What?" he asked.

"Pinky's Black Jack's girl, and I . . . I was afraid you'd take up with her and he'd come back to Blue Water and—" she stammered.

"Why would ya care if I 'took up with Pinky Chitter,' as you put it?" he asked.

"Black Jack will kill ya if ya do."

"Pinky Chitter's a . . . a . . ."

"A harlot," she said.

"That's one word for it, yes . . . and I'm sure Black Jack knows it. So why would it matter if—"

It matters to me, Cherry wanted to scream. Instead she told the second truth. "But yer one she might fancy enough to leave him for," she explained. "And Black Jack would shoot ya dead cold for it. So—so that's why I was in the barrel. I wanted to make sure ya weren't doin' somethin' that might get ya killed."

"You were in the barrel because ya were lookin' out for me?"

"Yes," she said. She thought his expression softened some.

"Well," he began, "I don't need nobody lookin' out for me, Cherry Ray."

But I don't want you with her, Cherry's silent voice screamed inside her head. Instead she said, "But Black Jack will drop you in the street if—"

"But since you *were* lookin' out for me," he interrupted, "I mean, hidin' in a barrel in yer pretty pink Sunday dress and all . . . I guess the least I can do is to thank ya proper." Cherry's eyes widened as he took hold of her arms with strong hands and pulled her closer to him. "And . . . after all . . . you are just about the best female shooter I ever did see. I guess that deserves somethin' as well."

She held her breath as his head descended toward hers. He meant to kiss her! He did! Her entire body erupted with goose bumps—the butterflies in her stomach increased a hundredfold.

"I-I ain't scared of you, Lobo," she stammered. "I won't run this time if that's what yer thinkin'."

"Oh, I'm countin' on the fact that ya won't, Cherry Ray," he said, his dark eyes burning with devilish intent. Taking her face between his powerful hands, he mumbled, "I'm countin' on it."

CHAPTER FIVE

Cherry didn't breathe but closed her eyes and tried to calm her trembling as Lobo McCoy's mouth lingered a breath above her own. Her lips quivered as his thumb brushed them in a soft caress.

"I came to Blue Water for a reason, Cherry," he said. "And you ain't it."

"I-I know."

"And I ain't some nice cowboy that'll do a little sparkin' on the porch swing and then ask yer daddy for permission to come courtin'," he mumbled.

"I-I-I know," she whispered.

"You'd be smart to stay away from me . . . to just stay outta my way altogether," he mumbled, his lips so close to hers she could feel the warmth of his breath in her mouth.

"I-I know," she managed to breathe.

"I'm only kissin' ya 'cause I want a taste of you . . . not because I like ya or nothin' like that," he whispered. "It's purely my manly desires. It ain't got nothin' to do with you bein' so fulla spunk or lookin' so plum cute when yer climbin' out of a barrel."

"I know."

For all the bliss washing over her, for the

bucketfuls of goose bumps breaking over her entire body, still she thought he sounded more as if he were the one needing convincing of his selfish, lustful character—not her.

And then—just as Cherry thought she might scream with the frustration of Lobo's teasing—he kissed her, pressed his lips to hers in a firm, demanding kiss.

She was inexperienced and too uncertain to respond. While her inexperience pleased him, her uncertainty did not. Lobo wanted to taste Cherry Ray's kiss the way he'd never craved anything in his life. And danged if he wasn't going to make sure that he did!

He allowed his hands to leave her face and travel caressively over her shoulders and arms. He felt her tremble—knew his touch was invigorating and reassuring to her. Letting his hands rest at her small waist for a moment, he drew her body against his, gathering her into his arms, forcing hers to encircle him. He was pleased with himself—for she did indeed melt against him and begin responding to his deepening kisses.

Cherry's blood ran heated through her veins, the hammering of her own heart ringing in her ears. Lobo McCoy was the most delicious thing she'd ever tasted! And kissing him—kissing him was far more wonderful than even she'd imagined.

As he held her against him, Cherry reveled in the feel of being in his arms—of the strength of his powerful body flush with her own. Furthermore, his moist, demanding kiss sent bursts of every beautiful color swirling in her mind. Quickly she learned to respond to him—to accept his kiss—to meld his with her own. And she'd never imagined such a thing! Even while reading about Oklahoma Jenny and Sheriff Tate, she'd never imagined Jenny was experiencing such intense and complete rapture.

In those moments, Cherry didn't care who Lobo McCoy was or why he'd come to Blue Water. In those moments, all she knew was joy, wonderment, and marvelous bliss!

Breaking the seal of their lips, he mumbled, "And that's why ya need to be more careful."

Cherry forced her eyes open, certain she would faint from residual delight and the sight of his handsome face poised above her own.

"Look how easy it was for me to get that kiss from ya," he said, holding her chin in one strong hand as his gaze lingered on her, seeming to study her face.

"That's 'cause I wanted ya to kiss me."

He was trying to make a point to her now—yet she suspected it wasn't the real reason he'd kissed her. She wondered if he would've kissed her had she been dressed in her everyday britches and not her favorite pink dress. Oh, how she wished she could wear dresses every day. How she wished she could catch Lobo McCoy's attention and kiss him every day!

"You wanted me to kiss you?" he asked, releasing her.

"Of course."

And it was the truth. Still, her real reasons for telling him the truth were not what he was about to think. She had wanted him to kiss her because he was beginning to own her—body, mind, and soul—because he was the most handsome and interesting man she'd ever met. That was the reality of it. However, she couldn't let him know it; therefore, she twisted the truth just a bit.

"You don't really think you woulda been able to kiss me if I hadn't wanted ya to, do ya?" His eyes narrowed as she continued, "I had my own point to make, Mr. Lobo. Don't think I wasn't aware of the fact you were tryin' to teach me a lesson . . . and I do believe you may have just learned a lesson yerself."

"That bein'?"

"That bein' that you might be just as easy to fool as ya think I am."

He was silent for a moment—seemed to thoughtfully consider what she said. Cherry tried to appear unaffected—as if she hadn't just told him the biggest lie she could tell. Oh, not that what she said wasn't true. She'd seen plenty of cowboys charmed out of a week's wages by the hussies working at the saloon. She knew a woman could lure a man out of just about anything if she had the know-how. Still, Cherry Ray had wanted Lobo McCoy to kiss her simply because she wanted him to kiss her. She was afraid he'd see right through her fib to the real truth.

"Yer lyin'," he said, a knowing grin spreading across his face.

"No, I ain't," she lied again.

"Yes, ya are," he argued with a chuckle. "Oh, not about the whole of it maybe . . . but in part. I think ya just thought all that horse sh—manure up right this very minute to try and cover yer tracks." Again he wagged a scolding index finger at her. "I've got ya all figured, Miss Cherry Ray." Shaking his head and still smiling, he reached out and took hold of her arm. "Come on, girl. It's time we kicked yer little britches home . . . 'fore ya find yerself in any more trouble."

Cherry breathed a slight sigh of relief. Sure—he'd figured out she was lying, but he'd seemed to miss the fact that it was true she had wanted him to kiss her. She wasn't even upset by the way he was marching her home, yet again. Nope! Those moments of being held in his arms, his mouth demanding she return his kiss—those moments were worth anything. Anything! Even the tongue-lashing she knew would meet her at the door when Lobo McCoy came dragging her home again.

"Shootin' whiskey bottles off fence posts?" Mrs. Blakely nearly screeched. "Cherry Ray! Shootin' whiskey bottles? On a Sunday? With a stranger?"

"She's a good shot, ain't she?" Arthur mumbled under his breath.

Cherry smiled as she saw the pride on her pa's face. Likewise, she smiled because Lobo still held tight to her arm. She loved his touch! She loved the way it felt to know he stood just behind her—that she could turn around and see him there—touch him if she had the mind to.

"Arthur!" Mrs. Blakely scolded. "Do not encourage her. This behavior just won't do!"

"I suppose it weren't the worst thing that coulda happened, Fiona," Arthur said.

"Well, I'll give ya that, Arthur," Mrs. Blakely huffed. "Trottin' off from town with a strange man that way. Do ya know what coulda happened, Cherry? Do ya?"

"Lobo ain't strange, Mrs. Blakely," Cherry said at last. She was tired of the scolding—tired of the constant nagging. "He's quite a normal-like feller. Now, Lefty Pierce . . . he's strange. He's got that one eye twitchin' all the time, and he likes pickled onions for breakfast. Now that's strange."

"You know what I mean, Cherry Ray," Mrs. Blakely said.

Still, Cherry grinned when she heard her pa stifle a chuckle.

"Fiona," Arthur began, "why don't ya see to supper? I'll take care of Cherry . . . and her smart-alecky mouth."

Lobo sighed. He did not envy Arthur Ray where trying to raise Cherry was concerned. What a little bundle of trouble! Stubborn, bullheaded, and with a witty tongue in her pretty little mouth, Lobo could only imagine the mischief the girl had gotten into over the years. He studied the back of her head, the way one long curl hung down her back. Immediately, moisture flooded his mouth at the memory of kissing her. Even now, as he held her arm tightly in his grip, not wanting to release her for some reason—even now he wanted to turn her to face him, drink the sweet flavor of her kiss again.

Lobo closed his eyes for a moment—tried to call a vision of his purpose to mind. He'd come to Blue Water for a reason—and the reason wasn't pretty little Cherry Ray. He straightened, released Cherry's arm, and looked to Arthur.

"I'll be on my way," Lobo said. "Just wanted to see she got home 'fore she stepped in anythin' else."

"I appreciate it," Arthur said.

"Afternoon, ma'am," Lobo said, touching the brim of his hat and nodding to Mrs. Blakely.

"And good afternoon to you too," Mrs. Blakely said. With one final glare at Cherry, Mrs. Blakely spun on her heels and stomped back to the kitchen.

"You still plan on lingerin' in Blue Water?" Arthur said to Lobo.

Cherry looked to her pa, recognized the threatening expression in his eyes.

"I do." Cherry noted the way he straightened his posture almost defiantly.

"Well . . . then we know where we stand, don't we, boy?" Arthur mumbled.

Cherry frowned as Lobo did as well.

"I guess so," Lobo answered. "Afternoon, Mr. Ray . . . Cherry," he said before turning and leaving the ranch house by way of the front door.

"What'd I tell ya about stayin' outta that man's way, Cherry?" Arthur asked the moment the door had closed.

"I didn't get in his way, Pa. I just sorta . . . sorta . . ."

"When you was shootin' with him," Arthur interrupted, "did you see him draw? Did he fire at all?"

Cherry frowned. It seemed an odd question. Hadn't her pa just scolded her for getting in Lobo McCoy's path? What did it matter if she saw him draw or not?

"Well, I did most of the shootin'," she answered. "But in the end, he did draw. Shot six bottlenecks off the posts."

"How fast was he?"

Cherry's frown deepened. Why would her pa be so interested in Lobo's draw?

"Tell me what it is ya know about him, Pa. Please!" she begged. "Is he an outlaw? I need to know. I need to know if—"

"How fast was he?" he interrupted.

Cherry shook her head in awe of the memory of Lobo's quick draw. "Fast. Fastest I ever did see."

"Accurate?"

"Shot all six bottlenecks off all six fence posts before I even had a chance to blink. He uses both hands to—"

"Triggers with his right and hammers with his left?"

"Yes," she admitted. "Pa . . . please tell me he ain't an outlaw! Please tell me he ain't here to join up with Black Jack and those boys in Blue Water."

Cherry felt fearful—terrified at the sudden vision of her pa having to gun down Lobo McCoy for some reason. It had been years since Arthur Ray had been faced with the need to gun a bad man down. Yet Arthur was a lawman—always would be. Cherry knew the only reason he hadn't gone gunning for Black Jack Haley was because it had never been proven that Jack was the murderer he claimed to be. But Arthur knew something about Lobo—something that made him want her to stay away from the man. Cherry felt guilt rise in her at the thought of the wonderful kiss she'd shared with the handsome man in the vaquero's pants. No doubt her pa would be furious, entirely enraged, had he been given any knowledge of it. Guilt was quickly squelched by the residual bliss her memory provided in the next moment, however.

"I told ya before he ain't here to join Jack . . . but that don't mean Blue Water ain't in danger, Cherry. Stay clear of that gunman. Do ya hear me?"

"Yes, Pa," Cherry mumbled. "But—but don't ya think . . . don't ya think that if he meant to harm me in some way . . . well, he's had his chance, Pa. I don't think he's of the same nature as Black Jack and the others. I don't think—"

"I ain't sayin' he'd mean to harm ya, Cherry. I'm just sayin' trouble's to his back and trouble's to his front, and I don't want ya caught in the middle." Arthur put one hand on Cherry's shoulder. His eyes narrowed, and he lowered his voice. "What'd I always tell you about a man who draws a gun like you seen that man draw his gun today?"

Cherry swallowed. Lobo couldn't be bad. He couldn't!

"What'd I always tell ya, Cherry?" her pa repeated.

"Gunmen are good with a gun for one reason," Cherry recited.

"That's right. Gunmen are good with a gun for one reason, and that one reason is killin', Cherry. So you stay clear of that man. I don't care how good-lookin' he is . . . how excitin' he may seem. He's a gunner and that's that."

Suddenly, Cherry felt hopeless, miserable, and disheartened. Her pa was right. Any man who drew a gun and fired the way Lobo did—well, it wasn't for the sake of herding cattle. Still, she couldn't believe he was an outlaw—she wouldn't believe it.

"Mind if I run out to the tree for one of my books, Pa?"

Arthur Ray grinned. He laid a palm against Cherry's cheek and nodded. "Go on . . . but don't let Fiona see ya. She thinks I ought not to be lettin' ya read them Oklahoma Jenny dime novels. She says they're rottin' yer mind."

"Thanks, Pa."

Slowly she meandered toward the old oak tree where she hid her dime novels. Maybe reading a bit would lift her spirits—take her thoughts from Lobo and his wonderful kiss.

Later that evening, as Cherry lay in bed reading of Oklahoma Jenny outsmarting Arizona Bill, her mind could not release any part of Lobo McCoy. His face, his confident saunter, his moist, heated kiss—every part of every moment spent with him played out in her mind. In her innermost, secretive thoughts, she even admitted to herself that his skill with a pistol made him even more attractive!

Cherry was suddenly aware of some commotion coming from the kitchen. Frowning, she put her Oklahoma Jenny down and wrapped a shawl around her shoulders. Stepping from her bedroom and into the main part of the house, she gasped when she saw one of her pa's hired hands laid out on the kitchen floor. It was Adam Cunningham. The back of his britches was blood-soaked.

"Pa!" Cherry exclaimed as she approached her pa, leaning over the wounded man.

"What happened?"

"Ol' Snort horned Adam."

"Strip his britches off, and let's see how bad it is," Fiona said, appearing from the other room. She was stripping an old petticoat into bandages as she approached.

"I sent Griff to fetch Doc Milton, but I figure we better get to this now instead of waitin' on it," Arthur said as he began to help the injured man unfasten his pants.

"Cherry, fetch some water, and get it warmin' on the stove," Mrs. Blakely ordered.

"Ya oughta put ol' Snort down, Pa," Cherry

cried. Her heart ached for Adam—the pain he was enduring was all too apparent on his grimaced face. "He's gonna kill somebody."

"He's worth too much in breedin'," Arthur said to Cherry. "You boys know to stay clear of him, Adam! What in tarnation happened?" he asked the wounded man.

"He broke through the fence somehow, Mr. Ray," Adam panted as Arthur finally managed to strip his pants off. "Me and Griff had got him back in and were fixin' the break, and he just—just came outta nowhere and got me."

"Cherry!" Arthur hollered. "Get to that water!"

"Yes, Pa," she said, hurrying to the kitchen for a bucket.

"Yer dang lucky he speared ya in the hind end instead of the gut," Cherry heard her pa say.

She hated when the hands got injured. It frightened her—brought to mind the pure fact of mortality—and she hated it. She hoped Griff hurried—hoped he brought Doc Milton running!

As she hauled the bucket of water back into the house and up on the stove, Cherry knew her Oklahoma Jenny adventures would have to wait. As she stoked the fire in the stove, she frowned. She hated old Snort! He was the meanest bull anybody ever saw—a Texas longhorn with the temperament of the devil—and she hated him! Still, Cherry knew enough about running cattle to know he was a valuable animal to own. She still hated him though.

"Well, I don't like him at all. Not one little bit," Mr. Murphy said. "Somethin's wrong when a man's that purty. Why . . . he's purtier than half the women in Blue Water."

"I say he's gunnin' fer somebody," Otis Hirsch said as he leaned on the counter of the general store. "He looks too awful independent to join up with Jack and his boys. Arthur Ray said as much, anyhow . . . said that Lobo character don't look a lick like he'd be one to take orders from the likes of Jack. Nope . . . I say he's gunnin' fer sure."

Cherry shook her head with disgust. There they stood—men who allowed a man like Black Jack Haley to roam free as a cloud—speculating about Lobo. Cherry swallowed, trying to appear as if she were interested only in the new dime novels Mr. Hirsch had just put on the shelf. The talk and speculation about who Lobo really was and why he'd come to Blue Water had only increased in frequency and drama since he'd ridden into town almost two weeks before. The fact he was lingering—seemed to be waiting for something—only increased the gossip. The gossip worried Cherry. Many were the times her pa related tales of lynchings—times he'd seen townsfolk take matters into their own hands instead of waiting for the law to arrive. Many were the times her pa had told her of frightened townsfolk hanging an innocent man. Cherry didn't like the talk she was hearing around town. Folks were frightened of Lobo because they didn't know much about him—and fear could drive people to doing terrible things.

"Carries a Peacemaker," Remmy Cooper said. "Looks just like the one Wyatt Earp carries."

"How would you know what Wyatt Earp's gun looks like?" Mr. Murphy chuckled.

"I read it in a paper. Last year . . . just after the O.K. Corral. It said right there in print that Wyatt Earp carried a Colt Peacemaker . . . and so does that Lobo feller."

Cherry smiled, knowing she'd shot whiskey bottles with the very gun the men were discussing.

"Well, whether Wyatt Earp carries a Peacemaker ain't the question here," Otis said. "The question is, how do you know this Lobo feller carries one?"

"Seen it in the saloon the other night durin' a card game," Remmy said. "I got a right good look at it. It says 'Peacemaker' . . . engraved plain as day."

"Engraved?" Otis said.

"Yep."

Otis shook his head. "It's worse than we thought then," he said.

"Why so?" Remmy asked.

"An engraved Peacemaker . . . it's a rare thing," Mr. Murphy said. "Costs a shiny bit too. Ain't many men walkin' that carry an engraved Peacemaker."

Cherry frowned. She knew Remmy Cooper played cards over at the saloon two nights a week—but Remmy telling the others he'd played with Lobo unsettled her. In fact, it downright made her mad! She knew if Pinky Chitter had made it clear to folks she thought Remmy Cooper was a handsome man, then she must be drooling like an old hound dog over raw meat at the likes of Lobo McCoy.

"Well, I saw more than that," Remmy said, lowering his voice.

"What more did ya see, boy?" Mr. Murphy asked.

Cherry stood still and strained to hear what Remmy was saying.

"Notches," Remmy whispered.

"Notches?" Otis asked.

"More'n I could count in the short time I saw his grip."

Cherry frowned. Her heart experienced a sudden pang. Notches on a pistol grip meant only one thing—kills. Frantically, she searched her memory—tried to recall the details of Lobo's gun the day she'd held it, used it to shoot whiskey bottles off the fence posts. Were there notches? She couldn't remember! She couldn't even remember if she'd seen the Peacemaker engraving. Oh, why hadn't she paid better attention to the gun? She shook her head as her thoughts answered her own question. What woman in the world would pay attention to the details of a gun when a man as handsome as Lobo McCoy was standing right in front of her?

"He rides a fine pony too," Mr. Murphy said. "I shoed his horse last week. It's a mighty fine animal."

"Hey there, fellers!"

It was Billy Parker. He and Pocket had just entered the general store.

"Hey there, Billy . . . Pocket," Mr. Hirsch greeted. "What can I do for you boys today?"

"Well, I gotta be gettin' back," Mr. Murphy said.

"Me too," Remmy added. "See you fellers another time."

Cherry smiled. Nothing broke up a gossip session like the appearance of innocence.

"Ma's plum outta sugar, Mr. Hirsch," Pocket explained as he approached the counter. "And I hate cherry pie without sugar."

"There's a lot of talk goin' 'round, Cherry," Billy whispered, stepping up beside Cherry.

"About what?" She figured the talk Billy spoke of was of the same sort she'd just heard.

"That Lobo feller. Folks is worried. They say one outlaw in Blue Water is already one too many."

"I don't think he's an outlaw."

"Well, outlaw or not, ol' Black Jack's gonna come gunnin' for him once he gets wind of what Pinky Chitter's been up to."

"What?" Cherry exclaimed.

"Did ya need somethin', Cherry?" Mr. Hirsch asked.

Cherry's exclamation had been louder than she had intended.

"No. No, I'm still lookin'."

"I think there is a new Oklahoma Jenny there, Cherry. I thought about holdin' it back fer ya," Mr. Hirsch said.

"Yes. I see it here," she said, reaching out and picking up the book.

Billy took the book from her. "*Oklahoma Jenny and Lawless Sue*," he read aloud. "You sure do like these books, don't ya, Cherry."

Cherry took hold of Billy's arms, fairly dragging him toward the counter.

"Will you save this over for me, Mr. Hirsch? I forgot my dime," Cherry said to Mr. Hirsch.

"Sure thing, sweetheart," Mr. Hirsch said, taking the book and placing it on a shelf under the counter.

"Pocket, Billy and me will be outside," she said.

Quickly, Cherry pulled Billy out of the store and onto the boardwalk. "Billy—what do you mean?" Cherry asked.

"'Bout what, Cherry? What's got yer tail all tangled up?"

"What's Pinky Chitter up to with Lobo?" she asked.

Billy shrugged. "I ain't rightly certain. Only that she's near to slobberin' on him every time's he's over playin' cards at the saloon."

"Why's he playin' cards at the saloon?"

Billy shrugged again. "It's what outlaws do, Cherry—sit around in the saloon, playin' cards, and waitin' for someone to pick a fight so they can shoot somebody."

"Lobo ain't an outlaw, Billy," Cherry said.

She drew in a deep breath—felt the hot sting of tears welling up in her eyes. Pinky Chitter? Jealousy burned through her entire being—scorching her heart, tearing at her soul.

"You ain't sweet on that outlaw, are ya, Cherry?" Billy whispered.

She closed her eyes for a moment, trying to dispel the remembered sensation of Lobo's kiss—his arms pulling her against him—the way his smile caused butterflies to rumble around in her stomach.

"I-I'm just sayin' he ain't an outlaw is all."

"Well, he better be one," Billy sighed. "And he better be good with that iron on his hip 'cause when Black Jack does come back . . ." He shook his head. "Pinky will win Lobo over one way or the other, and then Black Jack Haley will be gunnin' for him fer sure."

Cherry swallowed hard—demanded her tears

stay in her eyes, not escape over her cheeks.

"He's over there right now, and Pinky's tryin' her feminine ways on him," Billy mumbled.

"What?"

"He's over there—at the saloon—playin' cards. I just seen him through the window."

"What's he doin'?" Billy asked. "Is he a-smoochin' with Pinky yet?"

Cherry frowned. Pinky Chitter was the prettiest woman Cherry had ever seen! With auburn hair, emerald eyes, and skin as smooth and perfect as porcelain, it seemed to her that Pinky Chitter should've been married off and settled with some rich man out East. She'd always wondered how Pinky had ended up in a saloon in Blue Water, Texas, instead. Youthful beauty still radiated from the notorious saloon girl. Her smile brightened a room better than any candle or lamp ever did. Black Jack had claimed Pinky for his own years ago but had never married her. Cherry often wondered what kept Pinky as loyal to Black Jack Haley as she was. There wasn't a woman in the world that fell in love with an outlaw and didn't come to some sad ending, it seemed. Cherry's pa said Pinky stayed in Blue Water, lingered in waiting for Black Jack, always hoping the outlaw would settle down one day and marry her.

"She better keep her hands off him," Cherry mumbled as her thoughts found escape through her voice. Peering through the window into the saloon, Cherry could see Pinky sashaying around a man sitting at a table in the middle of the room.

"What's that, Cherry?" Pocket asked. " 'Cause it seems to me she's already done got her hands all over him."

Cherry frowned, furious jealousy rising in her bosom as she watched Pinky sit down on the man's lap. Pinky took the man's hat off and began running her fingers through his hair.

"Why are these windows so filthy?" Cherry grumbled. "Don't they ever give 'em a good wash?" She was frustrated. She couldn't tell who Pinky was flirting with, but she suspected it was Lobo.

"Y-you boys shouldn't be here. This ain't somethin' you should be seein'," Cherry said. She was angry at the tears gathering in her eyes. Lobo was a good man—she was certain of it! Yet good men didn't go letting saloon girls paw at them—and they certainly didn't smooch them in return or go up the saloon stairs with them.

"What in tarnation are ya up to now, Cherry Ray?"

Cherry Ray gasped as a strong hand took hold of her shirt from behind. In an instant, she was hefted to her feet, her boots grinding in the dirt as Lobo turned her to face him.

CHAPTER SIX

"You boys run on home," Lobo said to Billy and Pocket.

"Y-yes, sir," Billy stammered. He paused, however—looked to Cherry as if uncertain he should leave her in Lobo's company.

"It's—it's all right, Billy. You run on home. I'll be fine."

"Y-you sure, Cherry?"

Cherry nodded. "I'm sure. And don't go tellin' anybody we got caught spyin' . . . again. Especially my pa."

"B-but, Cherry—" Billy began to argue.

"She'll be fine, boy," Lobo growled.

"I'll be fine, Billy," she said, smiling. "Fact is I'm old friends with Lobo."

Billy's eyes narrowed. "You sure ya don't want me to holler fer yer pa, Cherry?"

"Oh, I'm sure, Billy. Whatever ya do, don't go hollerin' for my pa."

Billy still paused—still frowned. When she nodded her reassurance again, however, he turned and followed Pocket.

Cherry watched as Billy and Pocket walked away. Billy looked back over his shoulder at her twice, and she nodded with encouragement both times.

• • •

"What're ya doin' out here?" Lobo asked. He wore a deep, scowling frown on his handsome brow—an irritated, yet concerned, scowl. "Dang it all, Cherry! Ya don't go peepin' in saloon windows. Some shooter might think yer too awful nosy and put a bullet in yer head! What's wrong with you?"

"I-I . . . I was only—" she stammered.

"You were only steppin' in more mischief," he interrupted. "I swear I don't know how yer daddy sleeps at night for worryin' over ya. If you were my daughter, I'd turn ya over my knee and paddle yer behind."

"Well, I ain't yer daughter, now am I?" she said, glaring up at him.

She hated that he was speaking to her as if she were a child. She hated the men's shirt, trousers, and hat she wore—for she knew it was one reason he treated her the way he did. He'd treated her very differently the last time they were together—the day she was dressed like a woman and he'd kissed her like she was one.

"No, you ain't," he said, seeming to settle his temper a bit. "But, darlin', you gotta be more careful 'round town—'round men, especially ones the likes who linger yonder in the saloon. Yer daddy dresses ya up like a boy, and I don't know how long it's been goin' on, but I will tell you this—there ain't a man left in this town that ain't noticin' yer a fine filly."

Cherry's own anger lessened a little. Did he think she was pretty right then—even if she wasn't dressed in a pink dress?

"Ol' Black Jack and his boys are gonna ride back into town one day, Cherry," he continued, "and when they do . . . well, you just need to be layin' low more'n ya are."

"Black Jack only cares about Pinky Chitter. I ain't worried about him takin' notice of me."

It was a lie, of course. The fact was she did worry about it. Cherry had worried about Black Jack coming back to town ever since the last time he'd been there—the last time he'd been in town and tried to catch her when she was riding home one evening. She'd never told anyone about it—especially her pa—never told anyone about Black Jack finding her out picking berries near the creek and trying to force a kiss on her—never told anyone about how she'd barely made it to her horse after he'd chased her—how he'd tried to outride her before she finally saw the ranch house and safety. Cherry hadn't told anyone about Black Jack, and she didn't plan to. She wouldn't even let herself think on it. Her pa was strong, but he was older than Black Jack and no longer used to dangerous confrontation. She wasn't about to be the reason for her pa to go gunning after Black Jack. And so, she kept her secrets concerning the outlaw to herself.

"Well, the only thing Pinky Chitter's got on you is she shows more skin than she ought," he said. "Black Jack's seen her skin . . . might be he's weary of it. Might be he'll be wantin' somethin' fresh when he gets back."

"I ain't scared of—"

"I know, I know," he grumbled. "You ain't scared a nothin'. Ya've told me that a thousand times."

"I never told you that a thousand times." Her smart-aleck streak was stirred. "We haven't even seen each other enough for you to have told me a thousand times. Can ya just imagine how long it would take for you to tell me somethin' a thousand times? I mean, it'd take a month of Sundays for you to—"

"Listen, Cherry—" he interrupted, a rumble of frustration in his throat.

Cherry startled when a loud crashing noise erupted from inside the saloon. "What was that?" she asked, darting back toward the window. Maybe this was her chance—her chance to distract him from the fact she'd been caught spying, yet again.

She was pulled up short when Lobo's powerful grasp took hold of her arm. "Dammit!" he growled. "They've seen us."

Cherry gasped as Lobo pulled her away from

the window, taking her face between his strong hands.

"Yer gonna find yerself six feet under, Cherry Ray," he grumbled as he looked at her. "He's comin' out. Who is he?"

"Who's who?" Cherry asked in a whisper, trying to look back into the saloon through the window.

Lobo turned her face toward his again. "The old boy who was sparkin' with Pinky," he clarified in a whisper. "He's comin' out here."

"I-I don't know."

"Who is he, Cherry?" he growled. His frown was furious—as intense as was the fire in his eyes. "Is he a lawman? A rancher? One of Jack's boys?"

"I-I don't know! I couldn't see him good through the window! I . . . I thought it was you."

"Me?"

"What's goin' on here, stranger?"

Cherry was breathless as Lobo's hand went to her throat. Pushing her back against the outer wall of the saloon, he drew his Peacemaker and leveled it at the man who had just appeared.

"Ain't no concern of yers," Lobo said.

Cherry looked to see Fuss Ingram, one of Black Jack's boys, his hand poised above the gun at his own hip. Pinky Chitter stood next to him, eyebrows raised and a knowing grin on her face.

"Well, since yer a stranger in these here parts, I feel obliged to tell ya—that there's Arthur Ray's daughter ya got holed up," Fuss said. "Ol' Arthur's a retired Texas Ranger, and I doubt he'd take kindly to anybody who didn't treat his little girl just so." Looking past Lobo, Fuss looked to Cherry and said, "You all right, Cherry?"

"I'm fine, Mr. Ingram," she said as Lobo's grasp on her throat lessened some. "Y-you just startled him—us."

"Well, I'll tell ya this, Cherry," Pinky began, smiling as she studied Lobo from head to toe. "You sure did pick a mighty fine man to start up bein' a woman with."

Cherry watched as Lobo holstered his pistol. His hand left her throat to settle on her shoulder.

"Pardon me for drawin' on ya," Lobo said. "Just wasn't sure whether you was friend or foe."

Fuss smiled. "Friend . . . especially if'n yer up fer a game a cards."

"Thank ya kindly. Just give me a minute or two to . . . uh . . . to finish up here if ya would, and I'll be in right quick."

"Yes indeed," Fuss said. "You sure have grown up fine and pretty, Cherry Ray."

Cherry felt uncomfortable with the way Fuss's gaze lingered on her—with the way he smiled as he looked her up and down.

"We'll be seein' ya inside, stranger . . . whenever you and Cherry here have finished up . . . whatever it was you were doin'."

"You have fun there, Cherry," Pinky said, taking Fuss by the arm as they both turned to head back inside.

"I will, Miss Pinky."

Once they were gone and he could see them settled back at their table inside the saloon, Lobo breathed a relieved sigh.

"Yer gonna get yerself killed, Cherry Ray!" he scolded. "You'll probably get me killed in the mess of it too."

But Cherry's mind had quickly moved beyond any danger they may or may not have been in from Fuss Ingram. She'd seen the way Pinky Chitter had looked at Lobo—the same way a starving coyote eyed-up an injured rabbit.

"So yer goin' in there?" she asked.

"Well, thanks to you, I reckon I have to."

"But yer just goin' in to play cards. Right?"

Lobo's eyes narrowed as he looked at her. "I reckon," he said.

Cherry's heart was hammering like mad within her bosom. She knew darn well Pinky Chitter had her eye on Lobo McCoy! She knew darn well she'd tried to coax him into more than playing cards.

"Promise you'll only play cards," Cherry said. A strange sort of desperation was gripping

Cherry—gripping her as firmly as her small hands now gripped Lobo's arm.

"Why?" A spark of mischief rose to his eyes, and he grinned a little. "What? Don't ya want me spendin' time with Miss Pinky?"

"Sh-she's Black Jack's girl," Cherry stammered. Oh, how she hated the thought of Pinky Chitter touching Lobo! How she hated it! "H-he'll kill ya for sure if ya try to—"

"She's a saloon girl, Cherry. Seems to me if Black Jack don't care enough to drag her on out of here, then he ain't gonna be too particular about who she . . . spends time with."

"Promise me ya won't go spendin' any time upstairs with Pinky," Cherry said. Frantic, desperate, she reached out, clutching the front of his shirt with both hands. "Promise me!"

Lobo's grin faded, his eyes narrowing once more as he looked at her. "Cherry," he began, "you don't know nothin' about me. I'm as likely to be a murderin' outlaw as I am to be the preacher on Sunday. It ain't wise to think kindly on the likes of me. It ain't wise at all."

"I-I just don't want to see Black Jack gun ya down over Pinky Chitter," she lied. "That's all. He'll gun ya down fer sure if ya—"

"One of his own boys is in there slobberin' on her right now, Cherry. Black Jack don't give a mind to who does."

Cherry let go of his shirt. She took a step

back, certain she could hear her own heart breaking inside her. The ache in her bosom was excruciating—like nothing she'd ever felt before.

"So . . . so yer goin' in to her then," she whispered.

"I'm goin' in to play cards, Cherry . . . and only because you got me in a pickle in the first place with all yer dad-burned spyin'." He shook his head; his shoulders sagged a moment as he placed his hands on his hips and breathed a heavy sigh. "And now they're a-lookin' out the window at us. I'm gonna hafta make this good or else they'll think you were just spyin' on 'em . . . and me along with ya."

Cherry gasped as he suddenly reached out pushed her hat from her head and gathered her into his arms. Tossing his own hat to the ground and pulling her tight against the strength of his body, he placed a moist, lingering kiss on her neck. Cherry's entire being broke into goose bumps as she let her hands caress the breadth of his shoulders. She reveled in the feel of his neck beneath her palms, the softness of his hair between her fingers. Oh, she well knew he was just making good in front of Fuss, Pinky, and whomever else might not believe he'd been sparking with Cherry out behind the saloon. Still, there wasn't a thing in the world that could stop her from enjoying his attentions, no matter what the reason.

• • •

Hang on there, boy, Lobo silently told himself. *Just give 'em enough to keep their attention off her.*

But the feel of Cherry's soft hands lost in his hair, the sense of her small body pressed so willing to his, and the taste of the skin of her neck threatened to weaken him. She smelled like summer rain, tasted like sweet summer cherries ripe off the tree!

For a moment, Lobo considered on just giving in—on swooping her up in his arms, carrying her to a more secluded place, and having his way with her. But his honor and will were stronger than his desire—he hoped.

When he'd come upon Cherry and the Parker boys spying in the saloon window only minutes before, he'd been astonished by the fear leaping in his chest. What if Fuss Ingram had seen them spying? What if Fuss Ingram had found Cherry out there alone, unprotected? Cherry wasn't aware of her sweet, pretty allure. In her innocent inexperience, Cherry Ray didn't understand what men like Fuss Ingram might take from a girl who captured their attention—especially one who didn't have a husband or a beau to look out for her. Arthur Ray knew, however. Why didn't he send Cherry away from Blue Water anyhow? Boys' clothes did very little to hide her beauty. He had known that the first time he'd set eyes on her—standing there with that old dried-out wolf at her feet—he'd known right then how pretty she was.

"Promise me ya won't spend any time upstairs with Pinky," Cherry whispered.

Lobo kissed her neck again—this time allowing the tip of his tongue to taste her flesh as well. He felt her shiver in his arms, felt the goose bumps on her neck when he kissed her again.

"Promise me," she breathed as he bent and kissed the hollow of her throat.

He was near to losing control, he knew—but only near. Raising his head, he let his thumb caress the hollow of her throat—the place where his lips had lingered only a moment before—the soft, tender place above her heart.

He was breathless as she took his face in her hands, forcing him to look at her. The feel of her soft palms against his roughly shaven jaw robbed him of his breath for a moment. The blue of her eyes was mesmerizing—drew her to him like some hunter's trap.

"You won't go upstairs with Pinky . . . will you?" she whispered.

Lobo's mouth watered, wanting to kiss her. He had to get into the saloon—had to play a game of cards with Fuss—let the man know Lobo McCoy was a force to be reckoned with. Yet as Cherry held his face in her hands, as he savored the feel of her against him . . .

"Let me have a go at yer mouth, darlin'," he said.

"You won't go upstairs with her, will you?"

"No," Lobo said, swallowing the excess moisture in his mouth. "Now let me—"

Cherry didn't wait for him to ask again but pressed her lips firmly to his. Her hands slipped from his face, and she allowed her arms to go around his waist. He drew her tighter against him, his mouth taking hers in a moist, demanding exchange. This kiss—the way he kissed her, as if he'd been on the trail for weeks without water and she was some sort of cool, refreshing mountain spring—it was different than the first time he'd kissed her. This kiss was driven by pure desire—passion and near abandon. This kiss put Cherry in mind of succumbing to anything he might ask of her.

He had to be hers. She had to have him! As they kissed, Cherry realized she must own Lobo—own his mind, his body, his heart and soul. Her body filled with sweetened breath, felt light and alive as his hands encircled her neck. His thumbs traced her jaw and chin as he held her, kissed her with a kind of ravenous thirst—as if he meant to entirely drink her up! This was how women were ruined—by handsome, masculine men the likes of Lobo McCoy. As he kissed her, as her senses drowned in the heated flavor of his kiss, Cherry understood how Oklahoma Jenny's sister, Pearl, had been lost to an outlaw. Her body and mind were more alive, more stirred than they ever had been before! As her heart pounded with wonder, as goose bumps enveloped her body, Cherry suddenly owned a more humble compassion for women who had lost their hearts and reputation to such physically and emotionally powerful men.

"Th-that's enough," he growled, suddenly breaking the seal of their lips and pushing her away from him. "I-I gotta get on in there or—or they'll know we were bluffin'."

"But I—" she began as he bent and picked up his hat.

"There's things that'll go on here one day, Cherry," he said, pointing an index finger at her. "Things that have to go on here. I don't want ya in the way when they start up. Ya hear? You keep closer to yer daddy's ranch—closer to yer daddy, fer that matter—and quit spyin' on folks. It's gonna get ya killed."

Cherry swallowed, tried to catch her breath, to calm the wild beating of her heart. Lobo couldn't be an outlaw—not with the feelings he'd awakened in her! She was certain only a good man could've awakened her the way he had. Over and over she silently assured herself—just as she had so many times since meeting him—Lobo McCoy just couldn't be an outlaw! Furthermore, she had to win him for her own—somehow.

"You won't go upstairs," Cherry said.

"Don't you be waitin' around to find out," he scolded. "You get on home to yer daddy."

"Just tell me. Promise me ya won't go upstairs with Pinky Chitter. I won't leave unless ya promise me ya won't."

His eyes were narrowed, burned with an angry glow, as he took hold of her chin once more. "I won't. Now get on home to yer daddy, Cherry Ray," he growled a moment before his mouth crushed to hers in one final, fiery kiss.

"You won't go upstairs with her . . . or ya won't promise?" Cherry asked.

Taking hold of her shoulders, Lobo turned her toward home. "I won't go upstairs with her," he growled. "Now head for home, girl!"

Whacking her on the seat of her pants with one hand, he pushed her forward with the other.

Cherry took several steps then paused, turning to look back at him.

He shook his head and waved her on with one hand. "Don't you look back at me, Cherry Ray . . . unless you want me to be haulin' *you* on upstairs."

She gasped, her mouth gaping open in delighted astonishment.

Lobo chuckled and waved her on. "Go on, now. 'Cause of you, I gotta sit through a game of cards." He turned and sauntered away, around the corner and into the saloon.

Cherry smiled. She could still feel his arms around her—still taste the moist heated-flavor of his kiss. He liked her! She knew he did. Oh, she was certain his feelings for her weren't a drop in the bucket to what she felt for him—but he liked her. It was in his eyes, in his protective nature. Sure, she wanted his love—his heart—wanted to call him her own. But he liked her, and it was a start.

Picking up the hat Lobo pushed off her head before he kissed her, Cherry plopped it on her head and headed back to the ranch house. Along the way she picked a few wildflowers, inhaled the sweet fragrance of the grasses and trees, and thought of Lobo McCoy and his delicious kiss!

Lobo lifted his hat and raked his fingers through his hair. "Who's dealin'?" he asked, sitting down hard in a chair at the table. He inhaled and breathed out several deep breaths in an effort to calm himself. His ears burned hot with annoyance provoked by Fuss Ingram's knowing chuckle.

"Well, you sure ain't no coward, boy," Fuss said.

"Why so?" Lobo asked as Fuss tossed the cards around the table.

"Cherry Ray," Pinky Chitter giggled. "It takes a mighty brave man to fill up his needs with Arthur Ray's only daughter."

"Well, Arthur Ray ain't a Ranger no more," Lobo said.

He hoped nobody else at the table had seen the way his hands trembled when he'd gathered up his cards. Cherry's delicious kiss still lingered in his thoughts—the warm taste of her mouth still fresh on his tongue.

"Besides, I reckon Arthur Ray's near as dried up and useless as my dead granny."

"Ooh!" Fuss chuckled. "Looks like we got us a bad boy here, fellers."

Lobo looked up to the three other men seated at the table. Two of them he recognized as townsfolk. The other—well, he looked harmless enough. But looks could well deceive a man—he could just as well be another one of Black Jack's old boys as the barber's son.

"Ain't a man in this town who wouldn't give his left leg to do to Cherry Ray what I just seen you do, boy," Fuss said. "But there also ain't a man in town who'd go up against ol' Arthur Ray."

Lobo struggled to appear unaffected. He'd known it all along—whether or not Arthur had. Why did Arthur Ray keep his daughter in Blue Water?

"Well, she's too sweet a berry to leave on the bush," Lobo said. "And I ain't afraid of no weathered ol' Texas Ranger."

"What about outlaws?" Pinky asked.

Lobo looked up at her. Pinky smiled at him and

pushed the fabric of her dress down to expose one soft, white shoulder.

"What outlaws?" Lobo asked. "Ya mean Black Jack?"

"Fer one," Pinky said.

Lobo shrugged. "Ain't never met the man, so I can't rightly say."

"Ol' Jack's got twenty notches on his pistol," Fuss said.

"Twenty-three," Pinky corrected.

"That's right. Twenty-three. Three of them was Texas Rangers a lot younger than Arthur Ray . . . and with two legs to boot," Fuss chuckled.

Before Fuss could've moved to draw, Lobo drew his pistol and placed it on the table.

"Count them notches," Lobo said.

He watched as Pinky sashayed around the table. Standing next to Lobo, she leaned over the table and studied the gun.

Pinky's smile faded a bit. "Twenty-five," she said to Fuss.

"Them legitimate, stranger?" Fuss asked.

"Ya wanna find out fer yerself?" Lobo asked with a daring grin. "I do prefer even numbers, and this twenty-five's been a-naggin' at me for near to a month." Lobo handled his pistol. He let Fuss look at him for a long moment before smiling and slipping his Colt into its holster at his hip.

Fuss chuckled again. "I think ol' Jack is gonna

take to you right off, boy. Ain't that so, Pinky?"

Lobo forced a wanton smile at Pinky as she smiled at him and pushed her dress further off her shoulder.

"I'm more'n sure of it, Fuss. I know I already have."

Lobo reached into his pocket and retrieved five silver dollars. Tossing them onto the table in front of him, he said, "Let's get this game a-goin', boys."

"All righty then," Fuss said, fanning the cards in his hands.

Lobo inhaled a deep breath and tried to force his attention to the cards in his hand and away from the feel of holding Cherry Ray. She was a dangerous distraction. Black Jack would ride in soon enough, and Lobo couldn't find his own self agitated when he did. Yet maybe what bothered him the most was the confirmation he'd just received of every man in town taking notice of Cherry. It wasn't safe for her, and it didn't sit well with him. Maybe it was time he talked to her daddy. Maybe it was time he told her daddy why he was in Blue Water—no matter the consequences. After all, Arthur Ray wasn't a Ranger anymore. The old man had let Black Jack run free all these years. Surely he wouldn't gun Lobo down for telling him the truth. Would he?

"How much you in fer, stranger?" Fuss asked.

Lobo forced his thoughts back to the game. He

picked up one of the silver dollars sitting in front of him and tossed it into the middle of the table.

"In fer trouble where that Ranger's daughter is concerned, I'm afraid," he said, smiling and winking at Pinky Chitter.

As the other men chuckled and nodded, Lobo shook his head. *They think I'm joshin',* he thought.

CHAPTER SEVEN

Fuss Ingram was the first. Tucker Johnson and Lee Taylor soon followed. Three of Black Jack Haley's boys were back in Blue Water.

"Black Jack can't be far behind," Arthur Ray said. "You best get yerself a couple a men to up as deputies, Clarence."

From her hiding place behind the group of abandoned barrels between the general store and Mr. Murphy's building, Cherry looked over to Billy Parker. She saw Pocket swallow hard and Laura's face wince with worry. She really shouldn't have let the Parkers follow her when she'd decided to eavesdrop on her pa and Sheriff Gibbs, but what else could she have done? She knew three of Black Jack's boys were back in town. The day Fuss Ingram had seen her and Lobo together outside the saloon a week before had been the first sign of trouble. Jack's boys always rather trickled back into town one at a time. Cherry's pa said it was Jack's way of easing himself back into Blue Water—of intimidating folks gradually so nobody would put up a fuss about his return.

Sheriff Clarence Gibbs was the biggest yellow-belly of them all. Sometimes Cherry wondered why her pa didn't just drop old Black Jack himself. He could do it well enough—of that she was certain. Why didn't he just knock Sheriff Gibbs on his hind end and use his authority as a Texas Ranger to bring Black Jack in? Still, Cherry knew Arthur Ray must have his reasons—though she couldn't imagine what they might be.

"Oh, I figure we'll just lay low a week or two, Arthur," Sheriff Gibbs said. "Most times Jack's out and runnin' somewheres else before too long."

"That mess in San Antonio should never have happened, Clarence!" Arthur growled. "That dead Ranger and them two deputies Jack killed are on our heads. Mine and yers!"

"It ain't my fault they was such bad shots," Sheriff Gibbs mumbled.

"They weren't bad shots," Arthur said. "I've been told Jack shot the Ranger in the back. There hadn't even been a go-'round yet. That Texas Ranger in San Antonio was just a-walkin' into the barber fer a hair trim, and Jack shot him cold in the back. When two deputies saw it happen and ran over to see if the Ranger was still breathin' . . . Jack shot them too. Black Jack Haley's a murderin' coward, and we can't let him just ride back into Blue Water like he done built and bought this town."

Cherry watched as her pa shook his head.

"Nope," Arthur Ray said. "Things have changed all around. I won't let Jack Haley keep on with this business of robbin' and killin' and hidin' out in Blue Water. If you don't have the courage to face him . . . well, this time I will."

Cherry's heart began to hammer with rising fear. Black Jack Haley was a murderer! Cherry knew her pa had once been strong, quick with a gun, and near to invincible. But he was older now, missing a leg, and most of the time suffered a little with the shakes. In that moment, she wasn't sure her pa still had the upper hand on Black Jack. What if he confronted Jack—and lost?

She wanted to leap up from behind the barrel and beg her pa not to do it, beg him to send for some other help—lawmen that had a backbone. She wondered how Sheriff Gibbs even got to be sheriff! She had been younger when he'd taken over the position, and she couldn't remember how he'd done it. All she could remember was that ever since Sheriff Gibbs had become sheriff, Black Jack Haley had run Blue Water.

"You do whatcha have to, Arthur. You wanna tangle with Black Jack, then you go on ahead and tangle. Besides . . . I got this new feller, Lobo, to worry about. Folks is mighty uneasy with a new outlaw in town. Least ways we all know Jack. Jack ain't never hurt nobody in Blue Water—you know he thinks kindly on it and all that live 'round. But this Lobo feller? I don't trust him any more'n I do the devil."

Cherry watched as her pa shook his head in disgust. "Yer just about the sorriest excuse for a sheriff I ever did see, Clarence," he said. "Ain't nothin' more disgustin' than a lawman who won't uphold the law." Arthur shook his head again. "Black Jack will turn on this town one day, Clarence," he said. "He'll turn hard. Might be me he turns on . . . might be you . . . and I guarantee you, once he turns on one of us, he'll turn on the whole town. I guarantee it."

"I'll tell you what, Arthur," Sheriff Gibbs said, reaching out and placing a hand on Arthur's shoulder. "Just let it sit. Jack will ride off soon enough. Just let it sit like we always do, and everythin' will be just fine."

"Yer the biggest coward I ever did see, Clarence."

But Sheriff Gibbs was too busy trying to convince himself. "Maybe that new feller, Lobo—maybe he'll join up with Jack too, and then we'll all be as safe and as happy as kittens in a haystack."

"When yer lyin' out there in the middle of the street with a bullet in yer back, we'll see what tune you'll be singin' then. Won't we?" Arthur grumbled.

Cherry watched as her pa slapped Sheriff Gibbs's hand from his shoulder. Bracing himself on his crutches, he turned and moved back toward the wagon in front of the general store.

"Well, you have yerself a good day, Arthur," Sheriff Gibbs called after him. "And give yer girl my best."

Cherry looked to Billy—her heart still pounding with anxiety and worry over her pa's safety. As Billy motioned for his brother, sister, and Cherry to follow him, Cherry swallowed the large lump of fear in her throat. Her pa couldn't confront Jack! He couldn't! Jack was younger and stronger. How could her pa face him and win? Furthermore, if Black Jack Haley had shot one Texas Ranger in the back, what was to stop him from shooting another?

Once they were gathered behind the general store, Billy said, "Yer pa sounds awful determined, Cherry."

"I know it," she said.

"But don't you worry," he said. "Arthur Ray is the best Texas Ranger that ever lived. Jack knows it too. It won't come to nothin'."

All at once, Cherry felt the need to burst into tears, to sob long and hard. Every inch of her body longed for Lobo then—to be held safe and protected in his arms. She thought then of Sheriff Gibbs's telling her pa folks were uneasy about Lobo's presence in town. Not that she didn't already know it; the gossip and whispering and speculation had been going on since the moment he'd ridden into Blue Water. Furthermore, it had only gotten worse over the past several weeks.

Living with Black Jack Haley in their midst had frightened people into suspecting anyone new of evil doings. And Cherry still didn't know why Lobo was in Blue Water. He seemed to be waiting for something—or someone. What was he waiting for? Was he waiting for Jack to return? Would he join up with Black Jack and his boys? Certainly he'd played cards with Fuss the day Fuss and Pinky had seen Cherry and Lobo outside the saloon. Cherry hadn't talked to him since—though she'd seen him riding through town on several occasions and therefore knew he was unharmed. She guessed he and Fuss Ingram must have had a friendly game of cards in the end.

Oh, how she wished he'd ride up at that very moment—ride up, dismount, and gather her into his powerful arms—promise her everything would be all right.

"Let's go, Cherry," Billy said. "Let's go back to yer pa's place, and you can read that new Oklahoma Jenny book ya got from Mr. Hirsch to us."

"What's this one called, Cherry?" Laura asked.

Cherry forced a smile and pulled the book out of the pocket of her britches.

"Oklahoma Jenny and Lawless Sue."

"*Oklahoma Jenny and Lawless Sue*?" Pocket asked. "What's it about this time, Cherry?"

"I don't know. I just picked it up this mornin'."

"Well, let's get to it," Billy said.

Cherry smiled. She'd always imagined her own children would turn out to be just about the same way the Parker children had—adventurous, fearless, and full of mischief. She liked them ever so much, and she particularly enjoyed reading to them.

"Okey dokey," Cherry said, trying to ignore the fear still lingering in her bosom. "But just for an hour or so. Pa will skin me alive if I'm late for supper again."

"Afternoon, Mr. Ray," Lobo greeted as Arthur tossed a sack of flour into the back of the wagon.

"Afternoon, Lobo," Arthur said.

His heart was still hammering with residual anger. Clarence Gibbs was a coward and it infuriated him! Yet for all Arthur's talk of confronting Jack Haley when he rode back into town, he knew he couldn't—not yet—not until Cherry was settled somehow—safe. All these years he'd let it go, let Black Jack Haley linger in Blue Water, let him go on outlawing—all for Cherry's sake. Arthur knew he was older, slower, and with only one leg to boot. If he were to challenge Jack and lose, Cherry would be left all alone. Nope! He had to think of Cherry first. She'd be settled someday and then—then he could face Black Jack Haley.

"I . . . uh . . . I was wonderin' if I could speak with ya for a time, sir," Lobo said.

Arthur looked up—studied the young man's face for several moments. Something was on the boy's mind. Arthur figured there was more on the young man's mind than a young man should have to have there. Still, though he suspected he knew why Lobo McCoy had come to Blue Water, he'd sure like to know the whole truth. The expression on Lobo McCoy's face gave Arthur over to thinking the boy might be ready to tell him.

"All right," Arthur said, leaning up against the wagon.

Lobo glanced around them, swallowed hard, and said, "I . . . I don't mean to make it difficult for ya, Mr. Ray . . . but would ya mind if we talked where it might be a bit more private?"

"Not at all." His curiosity was piqued to the sky. As Lobo began looking around for a private place to converse, Arthur said, "You got a room over at the boardin' house, don't ya, boy?"

"Yes, sir," Lobo answered.

"Well, seems to me that's as good a place as any," Arthur said.

"Yes, sir. It is."

Arthur followed Lobo down the boardwalk to the boarding house. He smiled when the young man led him around to the back of the building and through a door there instead of using the front door.

Once they were inside his room, Lobo closed the door, locked it, and offered Arthur a chair.

"What's all this about, boy?" Arthur asked. He figured he knew—wondered why it had taken the boy so long to come to him. Pride perhaps. Or maybe just pure anger.

"I . . . uh . . . I got an awful confession to make, Mr. Ray," Lobo said.

Arthur fought the smile wanting to spread across his face.

"And what's that?" he asked.

Lobo reached into the pocket of his britches and placed a large, old Mexican coin in Arthur's hand.

Arthur chuckled and studied the coin. "It's a fine job. Who done it for ya?"

"A jeweler over in New Orleans."

"Lobo McCoy," Arthur chuckled. "I don't mean to steal yer thunder, son, but I knew who ya was the first time I laid eyes on ya . . . well, the first time ya told me yer name anyway."

"Well, who I am ain't really what I was meanin' to confess, Mr. Ray," Lobo said. "Though I'm a might certain that yer knowin' who I am ain't gonna make this any easier."

"Go on," Arthur urged. The hair on the back of his head prickled, and a dreaded sort of anxiety washed over him.

"Well, I reckon ya know why I'm here in Blue Water."

"I reckon I do," Arthur said.

The young man was agitated, nervous—not

at all the behavior that had made the name of Lobo McCoy so well-known among outlaws and lawmen alike.

"Then I reckon ya know how dangerous the town of Blue Water is just now," he said.

"I reckon I know that too, boy," Arthur said. Habit caused him to let his hand rest on the grip of the pistol in his holster.

"Well, it's yer girl, Mr. Ray. I know yer quite well aware of the mischief she gets herself into."

"But yer gonna tell me I ain't aware of the worst of it, ain't ya?" Arthur mumbled. Again the hair at the back of his neck prickled with dread.

"I'm afraid so, sir."

"I'll drop ya cold dead if ya've done anythin' the like of—" Arthur began.

"Oh, no, sir!" Lobo interrupted. "It ain't nothin' so bad as that. I just worry for her keepin' safe. She's awful curious, Mr. Ray . . . awful curious."

"Have ya told her why yer in Blue Water?"

Lobo shook his head. "No."

"Why not?"

The young man swallowed hard. "I . . . I don't want her thinkin' badly of me, I guess—bein' fearful."

Arthur's eyes narrowed. Cherry wasn't too good at hiding her thoughts. He had seen her feelings for Lobo McCoy. The moment he'd ridden into town, Cherry's eyes lit up like the stars in the heavens. He'd seen the excitement in her eyes the first time Lobo had come dragging her home from spying on him while he was bathing in the creek. He'd seen the radiance on her face the next time he'd come dragging her home like a bad pup—the day they'd been shooting whiskey bottles off fence posts. Both times the fear rising in him increased: he knew who Lobo McCoy really was, knew what kind of a life he led, and Arthur Ray hadn't wanted that life for his daughter.

Arthur handed the old Mexican coin back to Lobo. Lobo leaned back, returning the coin to his pocket. "There's a bit more I'm inclined to confess, Mr. Ray," he said.

"What's that?"

"It's—it's been twice now that I've . . . that I've . . . that I've kissed yer girl, sir," he stammered.

Initially, Arthur felt rage replacing fear in his chest. He saw the young man's eyes drop to the gun at Arthur's hip. "Go on," Arthur said, trembling with fury.

"First time was that Sunday we were shootin' whiskey bottles. Thought I'd teach her a lesson in bein' so trustin' of strangers," Lobo explained. "Then . . . then the other day . . . well, she got us both in a pickle, and I—I . . . truth is I couldn't help myself, Mr. Ray."

Arthur inhaled a deep breath. His anger was subsiding as understanding began to seep into his mind. Black Jack needed hanging. Arthur

Ray had spent ten years ignoring the fact of it—allowing the outlaw to linger in Blue Water free as he pleased, all for the sake of caring for Cherry, defending her, providing for her. In those moments, Arthur had begun to realize that someone else was beginning to care for his daughter—watch out for her, protect her, attempt to keep her from mischief and harm. It wasn't the life he wanted for Cherry—the life a man like Lobo McCoy led. Yet if Lobo changed—gave up the life he was leading in favor of something else—maybe then Arthur finally could confront Black Jack Haley—rid Texas of his murdering ways.

He studied Lobo for a moment. The boy looked weary—tired of running and chasing and knowing constant anger.

"There's a time in every man's life, Lobo," Arthur began, "a time when he comes to a split in the trail. If he chooses one trail . . . then his life goes on the way it always has. But, if he chooses the other trail, things can change . . . *he* can change. What's yer plan, boy? Which trail are ya gonna take? You gonna stay on the trail to Black Jack and the life that'll bring ya? Or are ya thinkin' on headin' off the other way . . . the way that might lead to me chucklin' at you sparkin' with my daughter instead of hangin' ya high myself?"

"Maybe I ain't to the split in the trail yet,

Mr. Ray. Maybe I just gotta do what I came here to do 'fore I can ride off in either direction."

Arthur nodded. "Maybe."

"I . . . I just thought ya oughta know about Cherry, Mr. Ray. I ain't slept a wink over worryin' she'll be standin' in the wrong place when Black Jack rides back in."

"I'll see that she ain't." His eyes narrowed at the young man. Yep. Maybe the time had finally come that Arthur Ray could stand up on his good leg, call Black Jack Haley out into the street, and try to do what he should have done ten years earlier.

"Thank ya for not shootin' me first and askin' questions later, Mr. Ray," Lobo said as he stood up, indicating their conversation was over.

"Yer lucky I didn't, boy. If anybody else woulda touched my Sweet Cherry . . . I'da shot him clean between the eyes. Yer a brave man, Lobo McCoy."

"She is a sweet girl, Mr. Ray. Full of mischief and vinegar . . . but sweet as they come."

"That's why her mama and me named her what we did—Sweet Cherry Ray," Arthur chuckled.

"You mean Cherry Ray?" Lobo asked.

Arthur shook his head. "Nope. Sweet Cherry Ray. Cherry's full name is Sweet Cherry." Arthur smiled. "Next time you catch her up to no good, you let her know you know her real name." He laughed. "If that don't bring out the temper in her, I don't know what will."

Lobo smiled and offered Arthur his hand. Arthur's eyes narrowed as he looked at the young man. This young man could be about to break his daughter's heart—scar her beyond recovering. Still, there was something in Lobo's eyes—the light of a man in line to change.

Arthur accepted Lobo's hand. His grip was firm and true.

"Thank ya again for not shootin' me, Mr. Ray."

"Yer welcome, boy."

Lobo closed the door to his boarding house room and went to the window. He watched Arthur Ray crutch himself down the boardwalk, back toward the general store. Wiping the perspiration from his brow, he shook his head—relieved and grateful to be alive. Arthur Ray may be older and missing one leg, but he wasn't someone a man went up against too easily, and Lobo knew he was a lucky man to have kissed Arthur Ray's daughter and lived to tell about it.

He drew his iron and spun the cylinder. Black Jack's boys were gathering in town. It wouldn't be long before Lobo would know what his future held.

Lobo left the boarding house, fetched his horse, and rode out toward Arthur Ray's ranch. No doubt there'd still be some old broken whiskey bottlenecks out near the east fence. If he was going to impress Black Jack Haley with his quick-draw—well, the more practice the better.

As Lobo rode beneath the hot summer sun, he couldn't stop the smile spreading across his face. He didn't want to.

"*Sweet* Cherry Ray," he chuckled. "Well, that's about the plainest truth I ever did hear."

Cherry and Laura held hands, following Billy and Pocket back to the ranch. It was a beautiful, fragrant day. Yet Cherry's mind and heart were still unsettled. She was worried for her pa. He'd sounded so determined, so sincere about not letting Black Jack Haley outlaw free and unpunished any longer. She knew it was the Ranger in San Antonio, the one Jack had shot in the back. She wondered—had her pa known the murdered Ranger? Was that what had his feathers so ruffled?

She thought of Lobo then, of his handsome face, alluring smile, and delicious—oh, so delicious—kiss. Why couldn't he just be a regular cowboy? Why did he have to be so mysterious and intimidating?

In those moments, Cherry wanted Lobo McCoy for her own more than ever! In truth, every passing moment found her more desperate to own him—more desperate to know his secrets—to know why he was in Blue Water.

Cherry shook her head. She would think about it later—all of it. For now, she'd sit down in the grass with the Parker children and enjoy her new Oklahoma Jenny. She frowned for a moment. What would Oklahoma Jenny do? Would she let herself be so unsettled, wait for Sheriff Tate to take notice of her? Of course, Oklahoma Jenny already owned Sheriff Tate's heart. Still, if she hadn't—if she hadn't already owned his heart, his love and devotion—would she sit in silence waiting? Nope! Oklahoma Jenny would walk right into Sheriff Tate's jailhouse, take hold of his coat lapels, and kiss him square on the lips. She'd tell him she loved him and demand he was her own from that moment on.

Cherry smiled at the thought of waltzing up to Lobo and doing the same. Sheriff Tate was a calm, chatty, rather cheerful man. Cherry shook her head in realizing what kind of a man Lobo was in contrast—secretive, watchful, and most of the time quite serious-minded. Still, he was wonderfully amusing when he was unguarded—as he had been when he'd seen what a good shot Cherry was. And she loved his protective nature! She thought of the times he'd scolded her, warned her about being more careful—it was ever so endearing. And then—then there was his kiss! Goose bumps broke over her arms and legs as she thought of the moist flavor of his kiss. Heavenly!

Too much thinking was beginning to cause Cherry's head to ache. She needed some rest. She'd read to the children for a while. There was always time for worry and wonder afterward.

"Hurry up, Cherry," Billy called. "There's a new family in town, and me and Pocket want to spy on them awhile before supper."

"A new family?" Cherry asked.

"Yep," Pocket answered.

"They's got three girls and two boys," Laura said.

"When did they arrive?" Cherry asked, for she had heard nothing of the new family in town until that very moment.

"Just this mornin'," Billy answered. "They're takin' over the boardin' house in town, now that Mrs. Coleman is movin' back east with her daughter."

"Billy thinks one of them new girls is purty," Pocket said. "She looked at him once, and he's still blushin'."

"Hush up, Pocket, or I'll break yer nose," Billy said.

Cherry smiled. A new family! That might make for some interesting goings-on—at least for a while. She wondered how old their children were. Did they have any girls her own age? She frowned. What if they had a beautiful daughter her age, just pretty enough to catch Lobo's eye?

"How old are the girls?" she asked. "Is there one my age, do you think?"

Billy shrugged. "All three of the girls look to be about the same years as me and Pocket," he said. "The two boys too. It's hard to say."

Cherry rolled her eyes. For all his spying and nosy ways, Billy never seemed to hang on to whatever information he might gather.

"Here, Cherry!" Laura exclaimed. "Right here under this big oak!"

"Did yer pa have that broken fence fixed?" Pocket asked, nervously eyeing old Snort. Old Snort stood just behind the fence. Even Cherry thought the enormous Texas longhorn seemed to be glaring at them. Her pa's prize bull was worth a big sum. Still, Cherry didn't care for him. Not one bit.

"Yeah," Cherry said. She thought of Adam Cunningham. She'd seen him just that morning, and he seemed to be feeling better. Still, she hated old Snort for horning the cowboy.

"Even still, let's sit back here—behind the tree where Snort can't see us too well."

"Fine with me," Pocket said.

"Now," Cherry began as the children sat down in the fragrant, green grass beneath the tree, "let's see who Lawless Sue is."

"As Jenny peeked through the window of the old cabin, she thought sure she smelled blood,"

Cherry read. "With a nose like a new hound pup and eyes like a cougar, Oklahoma Jenny carefully opened the cabin door and peered into the darkness."

"She's in there!" Pocket whispered. "I know she's in there!"

"Hush, Pocket!" Billy scolded. "You'll ruin the story. Go on there, Cherry. Who's in the cabin?"

Cherry smiled as she looked at Laura's widened eyes. So excited by the story, the girl had twisted the fabric of her dress into knots. She continued reading.

"One more step, stranger, and I'll blow a hole in yer gut the size of Texas," Lawless Sue said.

"That you, Sue?" Jenny asked. Jenny held her breath, kept her finger inchin' on her Winchester's trigger as Lawless Sue stepped outta the shadows.

"Oklahoma Jenny," Lawless Sue laughed. "I mighta known it'd be you who'd be ridin' out this way."

Jenny tensed as Sue leveled a pistol at her.

"Where's that purty sheriff of yers? Didn't ya bring him along this time, Jenny?" Sue asked.

"Nope," Jenny said. "I figure the likes a you don't deserve to look at a man so handsome as Tate is."

"Cherry Ray!" Pocket interrupted. "Is this gonna be one of them silly stories about love and kissin' and all? I can't hardly tolerate it if it is."

"I can," Laura said, smiling at Cherry. "Besides, Pocket's just mad 'cause the likes of Oklahoma Jenny and Lawless Sue never would find him handsome enough to speak of."

"That's a durn lie, Laura, and you take it back 'fore I paddle yer behind a good one!" Pocket shouted.

"I won't take it back 'cause it's true!" Laura hollered back.

"Children!" Cherry scolded. "Now you two settle down, or I ain't readin' any more. And don't ya wanna know what happens? Maybe Lawless Sue is gonna shoot Jenny cold in the back!"

"She can't shoot her cold in the back," Billy said. "They's facin' each other."

Cherry giggled, unable to hide her amusement over the children's banter. "Settle down now," she said. "We ain't got that much time left to read. I gotta be home before supper."

"Hello."

Cherry gasped, startled by the unfamiliar voice. "What ya'll doin'?"

Looking up to see two strange, and rather large, young men standing over her, Cherry frowned as Laura answered, "Readin' a book with Cherry Ray."

CHAPTER EIGHT

Cherry quickly studied the large young men. They weren't full-grown men—definitely still boys, but just barely. They had a glint of danger in their eyes that made her feel uncomfortable. Big, red-haired, and muscular, both boys looked like pure trouble.

"Who's Cherry Ray?" one of the boys asked.

"I'm Cherry Ray. Who're you?"

"I'm Tommy Baxter, and this here's my brother, Miles. We just moved in the ol' boardin' house in Blue Water," the biggest boy said.

"Oh!" Billy exclaimed. "Yer the new family in town."

"We been a family for a right long time, boy," Miles Baxter growled. "Ain't nothin' new about us."

Instantly, Cherry disliked the Baxter boys. They were trouble indeed—it was obvious. "Well, welcome to Blue Water," she said, offering her hand in a gesture of welcome.

Both boys simply studied Cherry from head to toe, smiling and chuckling as they did so.

"What're you?" Tommy asked. "A boy or a girl?"

"She's a girl," Laura said. "Are ya blind or what?"

"Hush up, girl! He didn't ask you," Miles barked.

"I'd welcome you boys to Blue Water, only I'm not sure I want to with the way yer speakin' to us just now," Cherry said.

"We don't need no welcome," Miles said. "We can go where we want."

"Well, you need a welcome from my pa to linger on his land like this," Cherry began, "and you ain't got one, as far as I'm concerned. So why don't you boys just head on back to town 'fore my pa finds ya out here."

"You ain't gonna tell us what to do, girl," Tommy growled. "We're from San Antonio, and we don't take to small townsfolk tryin' to give us orders."

"You get goin', or my pa will string ya up," Cherry said.

"Her pa's Arthur Ray," Billy said.

Both boys laughed, and Cherry stood up, intending to appear courageous and unaffected by their bullying. The two boys were bigger than she'd realized, however. She figured running might be the only choice left to avoiding them. Yet she knew Laura couldn't outrun them—even if Pocket and Billy could.

"Who?" Miles laughed.

"I mean it," Cherry said, attempting to sound more confident than she was.

All Lobo's warnings came flooding back to her.

She was safe enough from the men in town—the men that knew who her pa was and what he'd do to them if they touched her. Maybe Black Jack was different now, a threat to her the way he'd never been before. But nobody else would dare to touch her—nobody that knew her pa anyway, and these boys didn't.

"You get off this land, or there'll be trouble," Cherry said.

"You don't want to anger Cherry's pa none," Billy added. "He's a Texas Ranger."

Tommy shrugged. "So? I seen plenty a Rangers in my life—seen a couple a dead ones too. Yer pa don't scare us."

"Whatcha readin' here, girl?" Miles said, snatching the Oklahoma Jenny book from Cherry's hand.

"Give it back!" Cherry growled. She grabbed for the book, but the boy kept it from her reach.

"*Oklahoma Jenny and Lawless Sue*," Miles said. "Well, ain't that sweet?"

"I'm amazed," Billy said. "You boys . . . neither one of ya looks to be the type that can read."

Cherry gasped as Tommy reached out and shoved Billy. Billy reeled back but didn't fall.

"You boys get outta here right now," Cherry said. "Before there's trouble."

"Oh, there's trouble already, girl," Miles said. "And our names are Tommy and Miles Baxter."

Cherry was furious as she watched Miles send

her new Oklahoma Jenny hurtling through the air. She winced when it landed over the fence right next to old Snort. The bull was startled and shook his head with irritation. He let out a low, angry-sounding bawl and snorted. Cherry fancied old Snort was looking directly at her—glaring directly at her.

"That's it!" Billy hollered. "You boys ain't gonna come into our town and cause trouble!"

"Billy, don't!" Cherry shouted as Billy hurled a fist at Tommy's head. Her eyes widened as surprise overtook her when Billy's punch landed square on Tommy Baxter's jaw. Tommy reeled backward for a moment.

A frown furrowed his brow, and he took hold of the front of Billy's shirt, drew back a fist, and mumbled, "That was the last ignorant thing you'll do, boy!"

"Stop it!" Cherry cried a moment before Tommy Baxter's massive fist met with Billy's tender jaw.

Billy staggered back and sprawled to the ground. Cherry rushed to his side, kneeling next to him.

"You all right, Billy?"

"I-I'm fine," he whispered. Cherry could see, however, that Billy was hurt. He'd had the wind knocked out of him, and his jaw was already red and bruising.

"Come on, little feller," Tommy teased,

motioning to Billy to stand up once more. "You ain't had enough already, have ya?" Tommy readied his fist, and Cherry knew another punch would hurt Billy far beyond what the first had.

"You leave him be!" Laura cried, kicking Tommy Baxter square in the shin.

"Leave her alone!" Cherry shouted as Tommy shoved Laura to the ground.

"Cherry's pa will drop you two dead cold!" Pocket said.

"Cherry's pa? We ain't scared a nobody's pa," Miles laughed.

Miles chuckled and took hold of Pocket's arm, flinging him aside and sending him tumbling next to his sister.

"You boys stop this right now!" Cherry cried. "What's the matter with ya? Don't ya even—"

Her words caught in her throat as Tommy's hands suddenly encircled her neck. He was choking her—not enough to force her into a faint but enough to keep her from talking and unable to properly defend herself.

"Now, you," Tommy began, knocking the hat from her head. "Now you might be worth havin' some fun with."

"She's awful purty," Miles said, caressing her hair for a moment.

"You leave her be!" Billy breathed.

Cherry could see Billy trying to stand. She tried to shake her head at him—let him know he shouldn't get up—that another punch from Tommy Baxter might knock him clean out.

"I bet she's tasty," Tommy said, licking his lips as he looked at her.

Tears began to seep from Cherry's eyes. Tommy was choking the breath from her. She knew if she fainted, the Parker kids would be at their mercy. She glanced over at Billy, who paused in his efforts to stand. His eyes widened, a triumphant smile spreading over his face suddenly.

Cherry was puzzled at Billy's sudden change in expression—puzzled until she looked beyond Tommy and Miles Baxter to where Billy's gaze lingered.

Relief flooded her body as Lobo growled, "Welcome to Blue Water, boys!"

Instantly, Tommy released his grip on Cherry's throat, and she stumbled backwards. As Tommy and Miles turned to see who had spoken to them, Lobo reached out, putting one hand at the back of each of their heads and shoved their heads forward with brutal force. The sound of Tommy's and Miles's foreheads hitting together caused Cherry to wince and cover her ears.

Each Baxter boy reeled for a moment—but only a moment. Straightening his shoulders and clinching his strong hands into fists, Tommy Baxter growled, "Who the hell are you?"

Lobo's frown was that of fury, and Cherry could see the tight set of his jaw. "Oh, you don't wanna know who I am, boy," Lobo growled.

Cherry gasped as Tommy threw a fist at Lobo's squared jaw. Lobo stopped the punch cold with one hand, however, twisting Tommy's arm and shoving him backward.

"Get 'em, Lobo!" Pocket hollered. "You seen what they did to Cherry!"

"Lobo!" Cherry screamed as Miles threw a fist next.

Lobo caught this punch easily and shoved Miles back and said, "You boys don't wanna go around with me. I promise ya that."

Both Baxter boys seemed to pause. Cherry couldn't decide if the Baxters were threatened or not. Maybe Lobo's warning was sinking into their big, thick heads. Or maybe they were just considering on how best to beat him.

"Y-you look a might familiar, stranger," Miles said, his eyes narrowing. "Like I already knowed ya from somewhere."

"You don't know me, boy," Lobo said. "But if yer wantin' a closer look . . . then come on and get it."

"Lobo!" Cherry exclaimed. "Don't egg 'em on!"

"Ain't you noticed, stranger," Tommy said, smiling, "there's two of us."

Lobo chuckled, and Cherry's heart began to race with even more frantic fear as he raised his hands and motioned with his fingers for the Baxter boys to come at him.

"Come on, boys," Lobo said. "If ya think yer big and tough enough to treat a woman and children the way ya just did, then yer big and tough enough to take me down . . . ain't ya?"

"Lobo!" Cherry exclaimed as the Baxter boys went at Lobo—one from each side.

"Knock 'em cold, Lobo!" Billy shouted. He was on his feet now and looked quite recovered.

Cherry watched as Tommy Baxter reached Lobo first. Fists flying, the red-haired bully didn't last long. Lobo easily avoided Tommy's fists, landing one of his own to Tommy's face and causing his nose to bleed. Lobo turned in time to avoid Miles's punch, fisting him square in the nose as well.

Cherry wiped a tear from her cheek and tried to ignore the applause and gleeful shouts from the Parker children. Both Baxter boys recovered easily enough and went at Lobo again. Yet in the next moments, it was clear Lobo McCoy was finished with the horseplay. Reaching out and taking hold of Tommy Baxter's shoulders, Lobo pulled the bully forward and down until Tommy's head met with Lobo's knee. Rendered helpless, Tommy crumpled to the ground when Lobo released him.

Turning, Lobo caught Miles's fist as the younger Baxter threw a punch. Miles paused long enough for Lobo to growl, "You finished? 'Cause I'll break yer damn arm!"

Ignorant in his assumption, Lobo was distracted by the fist he already held, and Miles tried to throw his other fist at Lobo's head. Lobo caught this fist as easily as he had the first. Cherry gasped and Billy and Pocket cheered as Lobo then twisted Miles's arm behind his back and forced the boy to his knees.

"You wanna try that again, boy?" Lobo asked.

"No!" Miles panted. "No!"

Tommy had managed to get to his feet somehow and stood staring at Lobo and his brother.

"This ain't no way to treat folks, boys," Lobo said. "Whether or not yer new in town." Lobo released Miles, and he fell forward, lying on the ground for a moment, rubbing his sore arm.

Cherry wiped another tear from her cheek. How horrible! The Baxter boys were horrible! Wasn't it bad enough that Black Jack and his boys lingered in Blue Water?

She put one hand over her bosom in an effort to still the wild beating of her heart. It beat furiously in her chest from both fear and excitement. She studied Lobo for a moment, his vaquero's pants, the way he stood so strong and intimidating. The sheer sight of him caused goose bumps to run the length of her arms.

"Now, you boys apologize to these two ladies here," Lobo said. "And then you apologize to these two young fellers."

Laura suddenly wrapped her arms around

Cherry's waist. "I don't want them boys to talk to me," she said.

"That's fine, sweetheart," Cherry said, stroking Laura's hair.

"Sorry, miss," Tommy Baxter said as Lobo glared at him. "Fellers," he added, nodding to Billy and Pocket. It wasn't a sincere apology—it was hardly an apology at all. Still, Cherry wanted nothing more than for the Baxter boys to leave. She didn't care to hear them say anything else.

"Now, git," Lobo growled. "Unless ya want a couple a broken necks."

The Baxter boys paused only long enough to glance at one another before taking off at a dead run across the pasture.

"You all right, honey?" Lobo asked, hunkering down before Laura.

"Yes, sir," Laura sniffled.

Cherry was breathless, delighted when he smiled, reached out, and brushed a loose strand of Laura's hair from her cheek.

"You boys oughta get yer little sister home," Lobo said, standing and nodding to Billy and Pocket. "Get yer mama to take a look at that jaw there too," he added to Billy. He grinned at Billy. "You took that punch hard, boy . . . took it better than a lot a grown men I know."

"Yes, sir," Billy said, smiling. "And . . . and thank ya kindly, Mr. Lobo."

"Weren't nothin', boy. You did a fine job of

standin' up to them mean fellers." Lobo nodded to Pocket again. "All you kids did."

"But . . . but what about yer new book, Cherry?" Pocket asked. "D-do ya want me to hop on in there and fetch it fer ya?"

Cherry forced a smile and shook her head. "It ain't that important, Pocket. But thank you."

"But, Cherry," Laura began, "how will we ever know if Lawless Sue shot Jenny or not?"

"You run on home, honey," Lobo said. "I'll make sure Cherry gets her book."

"He's a mean ol' cuss, that longhorn," Billy said, glancing to Snort for a moment. He looked back to Lobo and smiled. "But I think you can handle him all right, mister."

"Thank ya," Lobo said.

For a moment, Cherry felt as if some strange fog had engulfed her. She looked to Billy—her young friend—thinking of all the mischief they'd gotten into together. She winced at knowing how painful the hit from Tommy Baxter must've been to him. She looked then to Lobo—the handsome, powerful man standing before her. She wanted to strip off her men's clothes right then and there—strip them off, pull her pink dress over her head, and beg Lobo to look at her and see a woman, not a silly girl dressed like a boy whose only friends were children. Not that there was anything wrong with children—Cherry loved children. It was just—Cherry realized in that moment, she wanted her own children! She wanted a man to hold her, protect her, and laugh with her. She wanted a man who would love her enough to marry her, settle down, and bounce their babies on his knee. Furthermore, Cherry wanted that man to be Lobo McCoy—nobody but Lobo.

She shook her head, dispelling the strange fog in her mind and telling herself to save her dreams for times when her little friends hadn't just been bullied and hurt.

"You all right, Cherry?" Billy asked.

"Oh, I'm fine," Cherry lied.

She was far from fine. She'd just been choked—nearly worse! She'd just seen three children she loved like little brothers and a sister beaten, bullied, and scared. She was far from fine! Still, she knew the Parker children would be better off getting home to their ma.

"You run on home," Cherry said. "You'll be late for supper, and then yer ma will tan all our hides."

"Will ya finish the book tomorrow?" Laura asked.

"We'll see." At that moment, she didn't feel much like reading about Oklahoma Jenny. "We'll be sure to finish it soon if we can't get to it tomorrow."

Laura smiled, seeming satisfied.

"We'll see ya then," Billy said. "Thanks again, Mr. Lobo."

Lobo nodded, and Cherry waved as they started toward home.

She could feel Lobo's gaze on the back of her head. She was in for a scolding—a big one. No doubt Lobo would march her back home, as he'd done twice before, and let her pa give her a tongue lashing.

"I-I know what yer gonna say," Cherry said. "You don't hafta say it."

"That weren't no fault of yers," Lobo said. It wasn't the response she'd expected from him.

"What?" she asked, turning to face him.

"I saw that whole mess start up, Cherry," Lobo said. He frowned, but she was certain he wasn't angry with her.

"You did?" she asked.

He nodded. "I was on my way out to them old fence posts where we shot the bottles the other day," he began, "and I saw you and them children walkin' over here toward the tree." He grinned and his frown disappeared. "I figured the four of ya was up to no good . . . so I followed ya. Tied my horse in them trees yonder," he said, nodding his head to the left. "I could hear ya when ya started readin' that book . . . so I sat myself down and had me a listen for a while."

Cherry felt her face blush crimson. He'd heard her reading *Oklahoma Jenny and Lawless Sue*? She was far more than a little humiliated.

"Oh," was the only word her mouth would speak.

"It's a very interestin' story," he chuckled. "I guess we better fetch that book so the little girl can hear the end of it one day."

Cherry shook her head. "I ain't goin' in there with ol' Snort. I'll just see if Mr. Hirsch can order another one."

"I wasn't plannin' on you goin' in there," Lobo said. He smiled and sauntered toward the fence.

"Oh, no! You can't!" she exclaimed, taking hold of his arm. He stopped walking and looked at her. His eyes were so warm and brown—so mesmerizing!

"Don't worry," he said. "I'll be quick."

"No! You don't understand. He's meaner than the devil! He horned one of Pa's hired hands just the other day—nearly killed him!"

Lobo looked at Snort—eyes narrowing. "Run on over there," he said, pointing to a small tree down the fence line a ways. "See if he'll wander over to ya."

"I don't need the book." Her heart had begun to hammer with fear once more. She'd seen what Snort had done to Adam Cunningham, and she wouldn't watch him do the same to Lobo.

"Well, I do," he said. "How do you expect me to sleep tonight if I don't know if Lawless Sue shot Jenny or not?"

Cherry smiled. He could fetch the book without

getting hurt—she was sure of it. At that moment, Cherry Ray was sure Lobo McCoy could do anything he put his mind to.

"Okay," she said. She released his arm and turned. "Snort!" she shouted. "Hey there, ol' Snort!" Yanking on a length of barbed wire stretched between two nearby fence posts, she smiled as the ornery old bull looked at her.

Reaching down, she picked up an old twig, tossing it over the fence at the bull. Snort took two steps toward her, and she started running along the fence line, away from Lobo and toward the tree.

"You old ugly thing!" Cherry shouted. "Come on! Come on over and just try to get me!"

Looking as if it had entirely understood the insult she'd hollered, the big Texas longhorn bull started toward her. She paused and picked up another stick. Tossing it over the fence, she hit the bull square between the eyes.

"Oh, he's mad now!" she called to Lobo.

As the angry bull started a run at Cherry, Lobo hopped the fence and raced toward the book lying in the freshly grazed grass.

Cherry gasped as Snort slid to a stop and turned. Eyeing Lobo, the bull swung his head from side to side. The broad expanse of the animal's horns was menacing, and the power of the animal wielding them was even more threatening.

"Snort!" Cherry shouted. "Hey there, old Snort!"

But it was no use. The bull's attention was full upon the man invading its territory.

"Lobo!" she cried. "Hurry! Please hurry!"

She could only watch, frozen with fear, as Lobo snatched up the book. Snort grunted low in his throat, pawed the ground with one hoof, and charged Lobo.

"Oh, sh—shoot!" Cherry heard Lobo exclaim as he turned and raced back toward the fence.

"Run! Run! Run!" she hollered as she watched Lobo sprint for the fence and safety. Snort was fast, however—not to mention furious! Cherry held her breath as the bull gained on Lobo. Certain she was about to see the man of her dreams impaled by her pa's prize bull, Cherry screamed as Lobo leapt, clearing the fence. Snort pulled up, snorting and swinging his head from side to side. One moment more and the animal would've had him.

"Don't you ever do somethin' like that again!" she scolded, stomping toward him. "You scared the life outta me!"

Lobo laughed and looked to the seat of his pants. "Now ya know how I feel every dang time I catch you 'bout to step in somethin'," he said, inspecting the long tear in the seat of his britches. "Looks like the fence caught me there."

"Yer lucky Snort didn't catch you or you'd be speared like a roasted hog." Leaning over, Cherry looked at the tear in Lobo's britches. "No blood," she said. "So I guess yer all right."

She startled when Lobo's hand suddenly covered the torn place on the seat of his britches. "Don't go lookin' there," he grumbled. "You'll see my drawers."

Cherry blushed, realizing she had been too forward. Still, she didn't want him to know she was embarrassed, so she said, "I've seen my pa's drawers plenty a times. I even helped when Adam Cunningham got speared in the hind end the other day."

"That's different," Lobo mumbled, frowning at her.

She fancied his cheeks were a little pink but couldn't decide if he were blushing or if they were pinked from outrunning Snort.

"Thank you for fetchin' my book," she said. "Even if yer a fool for doin' it."

"Well, I wanna hear what happens," he said, his hand still covering the tear in the seat of his britches.

"So yer wantin' to borrow it then?" she asked as Lobo handed the book to her.

"Naw," he said. "I don't have time for readin' such things. I figure I'll just behave like Cherry Ray does and spy on her the next time she's readin' to them kids."

Cherry smiled as realization hit her then. He'd been spying on her! Just the way she'd spied on him. Yep! He'd seen her out with the Parker children, followed her, and then sat spying on her while she read to them.

"I could read a bit right now if you'd like," she ventured.

It was bold—too bold, she knew. Still, she couldn't help herself. The hope of spending even one more minute in the company of Lobo McCoy had loosened the hinges on her tongue.

He grinned. His eyes narrowed as he looked at her. "All righty," he said. "But not where this ol' boy can see us. I think he's still eyein' up my hind end."

"Are ya hungry?"

"Why? You plannin' on feedin' me that book instead of readin' it?"

Cherry giggled. "No. There's a cherry tree not too far from here," she explained. "I figure I can read, and you can have yerself a little bite to eat."

His smile broadened, and she fancied there was a little too much mischief in his eyes. "Is it a sour cherry tree?" he asked. "Ya know . . . for makin' pies?"

"No," she said, shaking her head. "Sweet cherries—sweeter than anythin' you'll have all summer long."

"Sweeter than anythin', huh?" he chuckled.

"Yep."

"Then lead me on. Lead me on."

Cherry smiled and started toward the cherry

tree. She loved the cherry tree her mother had planted when her pa had first bought the ranch. In the summer, Cherry loved to pick a few cherries from her mother's tree, stretch out on the soft grass beneath, and just dream the hours away. She'd never shared the tree with anyone before—not even the Parker children. It was her special place of serenity and quiet. Yet she wanted to take Lobo there—to sit beneath her mother's tree and feed him some of the delicious fruit of it.

Cherry glanced over to see Lobo studying the back of his hands as they walked.

"My knuckles are already sore," he said. "Guess it's been longer than I thought since they was used in a fight."

"Thank you for helpin' us," Cherry said.

All at once, she was greatly humbled once more. She and the Parker children had been in serious danger—she knew they had. She didn't want to think on what might have happened if Lobo hadn't been nearby. "And thank you for fetchin' my book. Old Snort wouldn't enjoy it nearly as much as me."

Lobo chuckled and stretched his fingers as he walked. His hands hurt something awful! The red-haired Baxter boys had skulls as solid as rocks. He resisted the urge to remind Cherry of his warnings of the past—of what bad fellers might do to a woman. She'd learned her lesson.

He could tell by the sound of her voice as she'd thanked him, by the look that had been on her face when she'd seen him step up behind the Baxter boys. Still, fury rose in him as the vision of the red-haired bully holding Cherry by the throat pushed itself to the front of his mind. He'd wanted to draw his Colt and shoot the fool! Yet it had felt good to hit him.

He grinned at Cherry as she pointed to a lone cherry tree standing near several apple trees just up ahead. He shouldn't be there with her—he knew it. It wasn't safe for her—or for him, for that matter. But as he looked at the soft sway of her hips as she ran ahead of him, the way her hair cascaded over her shoulders—what man could resist sitting under a cherry tree with such a girl? Especially a man as haunted as he was, one who'd be moving on soon, one way or the other. He thought of the talk he'd had with Arthur Ray—about Arthur's implication that a man could change his life by choosing to ride a different trail. Lobo had already chosen a trail to ride. But in that moment, he wandered off the trail he was destined to follow and onto one that led to a secluded cherry tree and a pretty girl. It was just a short rest—a slight mosey off the trail he knew he still had to follow. Still—resting alongside the trail awhile—surely it wouldn't kill him.

CHAPTER NINE

"Jenny reached down and tore a length of cloth from her petticoat," Cherry read.

She quickly wrapped it around her arm and tied it tight. She'd need to get to town and have the doc dig that bullet out. But first she'd find Sheriff Tate and tell him what Lawless Sue had done. Jenny knew Sheriff Tate would ride out after Sue as quick as his pony would carry him. Fact was Jenny suspected he wouldn't even take the time to raise a posse. He'd be plum loco when he found out Sue had shot at Jenny. Even more plum loco when he saw Sue had hit her, and it wouldn't do to let the likes of Lawless Sue roam free. The law was the law . . . even in Oklahoma. Fact was Jenny felt as bad for the Cherokee on the reservation as Sue did. But that didn't mean a body could just ride around shootin' whatever moved. Somebody had to stop Sue . . . and Jenny knew Sheriff Tate would be that somebody.

"I think yer sweet on Sheriff Tate," Lobo said, spitting a cherry pit into the grass.

"What?"

"I think yer sweet on—"

"I heard what ya said," Cherry giggled. "And that's the silliest thing I ever heard."

"No it ain't."

"And why would I be sweet on Sheriff Tate?"

Cherry smiled, delighted by being near him. The sun was low in the sky, and she knew Mrs. Blakely would have supper on by now. Still, there wasn't a thing in the world that could've pulled her away from that moment—from sitting under her mother's cherry tree eating cherries with Lobo McCoy.

"I think you like lawmen," he said.

"What?" she squealed.

"Well, there's yer pa for one . . . and Sheriff Tate fer another," he said. "Seems you like a man who fights fer good."

"Well, what's wrong with that?" She was blushing—she could feel the rosy red of her cheeks. He'd guessed it! Cherry had always admired men who upheld the law. Sure, it most likely started with the fact her pa was one—a great lawman to be admired. Still, what was wrong with admiring lawmen? Nothing! But how had he guessed it?

"Nothin' at all wrong with it," he said. "Just don't give us regular fellers much hope, now does it."

"Well, the way I figure . . . you fight for good too," Cherry ventured.

She wondered if his kiss would taste like cherries now. If she kissed him at that very moment, would his kiss be warm and sweet like the cherries he held in his hand?

He chuckled and asked, "Is that so? How do ya figure?"

"Yer always haulin' me off to my pa, makin' sure he's raisin' me right, savin' my neck when outlaws catch me spyin' through saloon windows," she said. "Even bruisin' yer knuckles on bullies and runnin' from mean old bulls on my account."

Lobo laughed and spit another cherry seed into the grass. "Well, when ya paint me that way . . . I come out lookin' mighty fine," he said.

"I think ya always look mighty fine." She blushed again, astounded by her own straightforwardness.

"Do ya now?" he asked, his eyes narrowing as he looked at her.

Suddenly, she felt herself coward down. She'd revealed too much to him. "Though ya do need a bit more practice at spittin' cherry pits," she said. She set her book aside, tossed a cherry up in the air and easily caught it in her mouth. Pulling the stem out of her mouth, she flicked it at Lobo as she tore the fruit away from the pit with her teeth. When she'd swallowed the sweet part, she spit the pit high in the air—watching as it arched and fell to the ground some ways away.

"See there?" she asked. "Now let's see ya beat that!"

Lobo tore the stem off one of the cherries in his hand, and put the cherry in his mouth. In a moment, he spit the pit high into the air, but not as high as Cherry had. The pit didn't fly as far, and Cherry giggled.

"Looks like I need more practice at pit spittin'."

Cherry giggled. "Well, we all need more practice at somethin' . . . now don't we?"

"Like what?"

Cherry shrugged. "Like not gettin' caught when we're spyin' on handsome strangers." She smiled at him—momentarily mesmerized by his attractive manner and appearance. Her heart began to beat a bit faster, and she felt overly warm all of a sudden.

"You think I'm handsome?"

Cherry blushed. "I wouldn't be spyin' on ya as often as I do if ya weren't," she admitted.

"What else do ya need practice at?" he asked, attempting to spit another pit the distance Cherry had.

Cherry looked away from him for a moment—a sudden feeling of discouragement washing over her. "Lookin' like a woman instead of a man, I guess," she said.

"Naw. You got that one licked."

"Really?"

Oh, how desperately she wanted him to see her as a woman! She felt ridiculous sitting there with him—dressed in britches and one of her pa's old shirts. Oh, how she wished she were wearing the pink dress she'd worn the day he'd kissed her out near the old fence posts. Maybe then she could tempt him—somehow tease him into kissing her once more.

Lobo chuckled. "What?" he asked. "Ain't you got a mirror?" He winked at her as he stood up, putting another cherry in his mouth.

"Lobo?" she asked, standing as well and watching as he spit another pit high into the air.

"Yeah?"

"Why—why do you spend time with me?" The question was out of her mouth before she could think better of asking it.

"Well, I do wonder what ya did . . . how ya kept outta trouble before I rode into town," he said.

"So yer just keepin' me outta trouble?" she asked. She felt her heart sink to the bottom of her stomach.

He looked at her and smiled. "Way I see it . . . I gotcha into more trouble than I ever gotcha out of."

"How do ya figure that?"

He moved closer to her, and her heart began to pound with a wonderful type of excitement.

"Well," he began, "take this cherry here." He held a cherry between his thumb and forefinger—held it in front of her face for her to look at. "It's an unusual cherry—different than the others I been eatin'."

"It's just a cherry. How's it different from the others?"

"Well, if ya taste it, you'll see what I mean."

Cherry giggled, tried to ignore the goose bumps breaking over her arms, the butterflies taking flight in her stomach as he pressed the cherry to her lips.

"Go on," he mumbled. "Taste it."

Lobo gently pushed the cherry into Cherry's mouth as her lips parted. Chewing the fruit she'd pulled away from the pit with her teeth, she said, "It doesn't taste any different to me."

"Is that so?" he asked a moment before his mouth crushed to her own.

Cherry gasped, elated by the feel of his warm, demanding kiss! A moment later, he chuckled, broke the seal of their lips, and turned his head to spit out the cherry pit he'd retrieved from Cherry's mouth during their kiss.

"Now you tell me," he mumbled, gathering her into his arms, "you tell me, Sweet Cherry Ray, ain't that the best cherry ya ever did taste?"

Cherry felt her knees give way—heard Lobo chuckle as he steadied her in his embrace. "Sweet Cherry Ray," he breathed as his gaze lingered on her face—her eyes—her mouth. He raised one hand to her face, caressing her lips with the tips of his fingers.

"In all my life, I never heard a name fit a girl any better," he said. His eyes were warm, inviting, and filled with mischief.

"Wh-who told you my name was Sweet

Cherry?" she asked, breathless and weak in his arms.

Ignoring her question, Lobo simply smiled and mumbled, "Mmm mmmm! Nothin' like the taste of a pretty Sweet Cherry on a summer's day."

Lobo McCoy kissed her then—kissed Cherry Ray until she wasn't sure whether she was awake or dreaming! Moist, heated, and lingering were the kisses he rained on her. The way he held her in his arms—powerful, demanding, and protective—his slightest touch was breathtaking! His kiss, his caress, the feel of his jaw working to weave a spell of pleasure and enchantment around her—she was lost to him! She was lost to his every will and whim! Wrapped in the bliss of being owned by him—heart, mind, body, and soul—Cherry feared she might not have the strength to leave him—ever!

She felt tears welling in her eyes as she realized in those moments, she was in love—hopelessly in love—with a man she knew nothing about! Cherry's heart beat frantic in her bosom—she felt her body trembling as the knowledge rinsed over her. Yes! Yes, she'd known almost at once that she'd wanted Lobo McCoy, wanted his heart, to own him and be owned by him. Yet it was only in those moments, as his mouth demanded hers return his driven and delicious kisses—it was only in those moments that Cherry Ray realized how truly in danger she was.

Lobo broke their kiss abruptly. Pulling her against his body, he whispered in her ear, "I ain't for you, Cherry. I ain't the kind of man you need. This is all I can ever give ya . . . a little sparkin' out under a tree, or—"

"I-I don't care," Cherry interrupted. "I don't care. I know I'm not what a man like you wants in a woman. I know I could never be . . . but I don't care! Yer the only thing in this world that has ever made me feel so completely happy and alive. Even if it's for just this minute . . . I'd rather have you for one minute than not at all!"

It was enough! With her assurance she would not keep him from whatever trail he was on, Cherry's mouth flooded with moisture and desire as Lobo kissed her again.

Was this what freedom was? Was this what it looked like, smelled like? Was the wonderful feeling of holding Cherry in his arms, kissing her the way he'd only dreamed of kissing a woman—was this where the change in the trail might lead?

Lobo fought the ideas coming to his mind—thoughts of settling, of giving up what he'd come to Blue Water to do. Visions of Cherry reading to children under a tree, dressed up in a pink dress for Sunday service—overwhelming visions of her smile, her touch, her laughter washed over Lobo like a lovely mountain waterfall.

He swore to himself that nothing in heaven or

on the green, green earth tasted as good as Sweet Cherry Ray did—nothing smelled as fragrant, fit as perfectly in his arms. A man could choose another trail—if Cherry Ray was at the end of it. Maybe her daddy had been right. Maybe he could give up his planned meeting with Black Jack Haley. Maybe he could forget the reason he'd come to Blue Water—trade it for a much, much better reason.

Yet another vision crept into his mind, tainting his dreams. His past was behind him—too close behind him—and it could mean danger for the beautiful girl he held in his arms. He tried to stop kissing her—tried to push her away—keep himself from drinking in the warm flavor of her mouth, but he couldn't. One minute more—just one. One more minute of holding her, kissing her, dreaming she could belong to him. One more moment and he'd leave her—give her up to keep her safe.

The shots rang out, and Lobo's body jerked with the force and pain of the bullets riddling his body. Cherry screamed as Lobo pushed her—pushed her back against the tree—protecting her from the bullets cutting the air and him.

"Oof!" he panted as another shot rang out—as another bullet hit him.

Cherry couldn't breathe as she watched Lobo draw his pistol and turn to face whomever was shooting at them. She screamed as she saw two red-haired men on horseback. Lobo hammered and triggered his pistol, and one of the men lurched and fell off his horse. The other man seemed to pause, looked at Cherry and then to Lobo, turned his horse, and rode off at a mad gallop.

Lobo reeled back, staggered, and dropped to his knees in the grass beneath the cherry tree.

"I-I shoulda never looked at you . . . never touched you," he panted.

Trembling and sobbing, Cherry saw the blood soaking Lobo's shirt at the right shoulder and arm—at his right leg and right hip. Trying to keep from screaming—from fainting—Cherry counted the wounds. Five! Five bullets had struck him—at least five!

"I . . . I gotta get ya back to yer pa," he panted as he stood and holstered his gun. He stumbled, his knees buckling, nearly sending him to the ground once more.

"We've got to get you to Doc Milton, Lobo!" she cried.

He shook his head. "Y-you get to yer pa," he breathed. "I can take care of myself." Again he shook his head as if trying to wake himself. He reached out, taking her face between his hands. "You'll be safe with yer pa," he said.

Cherry saw the movement—saw the man who had fallen from his horse sit up in the grass. As the man leveled a rifle at Lobo's back, Cherry reached over, drawing Lobo's pistol from the holster at his hip. Her shot rang out first, and the man fell backward into the grass. He groaned where he lay, but Cherry didn't care. He'd ambushed Lobo McCoy—the man she loved— and Cherry didn't care if he bled to death where he lay in her pa's pasture.

"Cherry!" Lobo growled, taking the pistol from her hand and holstering it once more. "You need to get to yer pa!"

"I'll get you to the doctor," she said, taking his arm and draping it over her shoulder. "Then I'll get to my pa!"

Lobo's blood was seemingly everywhere! Cherry had never seen so much. And he was weak. No matter how he scolded and growled as they rode to town on the back of the horse belonging to the man who now lay bleeding out in Arthur Ray's pasture, Cherry ignored him. He'd die if he wasn't tended to. He'd die! Never had she known such fear—such overwhelming fear!

"Here, Cherry," he said, suddenly ripping the leather from her hand and reining in before the jailhouse. "Drop me here and get on back home." He tried to dismount but collapsed to the ground. Instantly, Cherry dismounted, took hold of his arms, and helped him as he struggled to stand.

Lobo pushed at her and growled, "Get away from me before I get ya killed!"

But she followed him, helped him as he stumbled into the jailhouse.

"What in tarnation?" Sheriff Gibbs exclaimed as Lobo stumbled into the room. "Cherry Ray! What're you doin' with this outlaw?"

"There's a man out in the pasture . . . in Arthur Ray's south pasture," Lobo stammered.

"Lobo!" she cried. "We need to get you to the—"

"He tried to gun me down," Lobo said.

"Looks to me like he *did*," Sheriff Gibbs said.

Cherry's hand stung with the force of the slap she delivered to Sheriff Gibbs. The coward stood stunned into silence.

Lobo looked to Cherry. Even for his weakness and the pain he was enduring, he grinned at her—nodding his approval of the hard slap she'd delivered to Sheriff Gibbs's cheek.

"Get out there and drag him in here so I can talk to him once I'm patched up," Lobo said.

"I got a better idea, stranger," Sheriff Gibbs said. "How about I put you in one of these here cells! I ain't heard back yet . . . but I'm sure there's a price on your head, and I aim to claim it!"

Cherry gasped as Lobo's fist met with Sheriff Gibbs's nose. Reaching into his pocket while Sheriff Gibbs was pressing his hands to his face to ease the pain and bleeding, Lobo withdrew what looked to be a coin. He tossed it on the desk in front of the sheriff.

"Lobo McCoy," he breathed. "Texas Ranger . . . and yer a damn fool!"

Cherry sobbed as Lobo's strong body gave into the need for unconsciousness. Dropping to her knees, she pressed her ear against his chest. His heart still beat; his breath, though shallow, told her he still lived.

As if sent by heaven's angels themselves, Billy Parker burst into the room.

"Cherry!" he hollered. "Wh-what happened? I saw ya ride in with Lobo and—"

"Texas Ranger?" Sheriff Gibbs breathed as he picked up the old Mexican coin fashioned into the familiar badge of a Texas Ranger.

"Take that horse just outside, Billy," Cherry instructed. "Take that horse and ride over to Doc Milton's. Tell him Lobo's been shot, and send him here. Then ride home and fetch my pa. Tell him Lobo McCoy's been shot . . . bad! He'll know what to do."

Without another word, Billy nodded and raced outside.

"There were two of 'em," Cherry said to Sheriff Gibbs. "Two men shot him down. One's in the pasture . . . dead, I hope! The other rode off toward town."

Sheriff Gibbs stood astonished into silence.

"Lobo McCoy . . ." he whispered. "Right here in Blue Water."

Cherry shook her head. Reaching up, she snatched Lobo's badge from Sheriff Gibbs and slipped it into the pocket of her britches. Wiping more tears from her face, she stood and bolted the jailhouse door. She hurried to the gun rack nearby and pulled a Winchester rifle from its place.

"Now—now you be careful, Cherry Ray," Sheriff Gibbs stammered. "That there gun's loaded."

Leveling the rifle at the coward standing before her, Cherry whispered, "I know."

CHAPTER TEN

"N-now, Cherry," Sheriff Gibbs stammered. "Yer upset. Ya ain't thinkin' clear."

"Set a fire in that stove, and get the water in that kettle to heatin' up, Sheriff," she said, ignoring the tears streaming over her cheeks.

When the sheriff didn't move, Cherry steadied the rifle and nodded toward the potbellied stove and kettle in one corner of the room.

"Now, Cherry . . . I'm the law 'round here."

"Yer no lawman," Cherry said. "Yer just a coward someone was dumb enough to give a badge over to. Now stoke that fire. Doc Milton will need hot water when he gets here."

"Now, Cherry—" he said, shaking his head.

"Lobo shot the feller in the pasture off his horse, Sheriff . . . but I'm the one who shot him when he tried to get up. So don't think I won't shoot a man who refuses to help Lobo now . . . any man."

Cherry shook her head as she saw Sheriff Gibbs reach for the gun at his hip. "Don't even consider on that," she said. "'Cause if I don't shoot ya dead, my pa surely will. Now set that fire."

Sheriff Gibbs swallowed hard and nodded. Slowly, he turned and went to the stove. She glanced down at Lobo—so still and lifeless on the jailhouse floor.

"I didn't know he was a Ranger, Cherry," Sheriff Gibbs said as he worked on setting a fire. "Them new boys in town—them Baxter boys—they showed up here all bloodied and beat. They said they was out walkin' when a man called Lobo took to beatin' 'em. They had their pa and his brother with 'em."

Cherry felt her eyes narrow as fury blazed hot through her whole body.

"And bein' the coward that ya are . . . you sent 'em out after us," she said.

"I . . . I told 'em Lobo was a stranger, that we didn't know much about him . . . so I couldn't rightly bring him in when—"

"You told him Lobo was an outlaw, and you sent them ridin' after him with the idea of a reward bein' offered," she said through clenched teeth. "I know you better than you think I do, Sheriff. I've watched you hidin' in the corners of this town for years!"

"Well, he shouldn'ta beat them two boys!" Sheriff Gibbs shouted, turning to face Cherry. "It weren't right, him beatin' on them two innocent—"

"Innocent?" she cried. "Them two boys was bullyin' the Parker children and me! One of them hit Billy Parker so hard I thought he'd busted his jaw. They pushed Pocket and Laura around . . .

and then the biggest one tried to choke the life outta me! I don't know what woulda happened if Lobo hadn't been right there to protect us! You idiot! You idiot! How did you ever get that badge?"

There was a knock on the door, and Doc Milton hollered, "It's me, Sheriff. Let me on in, would ya?"

Sheriff Gibbs started toward the door.

"Drop yer gun at my feet first," Cherry ordered.

"Now, Cherry—"

"Do it! Drop it now!"

Sheriff Gibbs shook his head. Slowly he slipped his gun from the holster and leaned over, laying it at Cherry's feet. Cherry kicked the pistol, sending it sliding under the desk and out of Sheriff Gibbs's reach.

"Now open that door and let Doc Milton in," she said.

Sheriff Gibbs's chest rose and fell with the labored breathing of barely restrained anger. Still, as Cherry kept her rifle leveled at him, he went to the door and drew the bolt.

"Billy Parker says some feller got shot," Doc Milton said.

"Close the door and bolt it," Cherry said, glaring at Sheriff Gibbs.

"Cherry Ray!" Doc Milton exclaimed. "What in tarnation do ya think yer doin'?"

"Lobo McCoy's a Texas Ranger, Doc," Cherry

explained. "Two men ambushed us and shot him—five times as near as I can count when I'm so rattled up."

"A Texas Ranger?" Doc Milton breathed as his attention fell to the man sprawled on the floor.

"Fact is, I think Sheriff Gibbs can be held responsible . . . bein' that he sent the two men who shot him," Cherry said.

"Now wait just a doggone minute, Cherry," Sheriff Gibbs began.

"Get back there," she ordered. "Back into one of the jail cells."

"What?" he hollered.

"Until my pa gets here, yer gonna stay locked up where you can't hurt anybody else."

Striding toward him, Cherry let the muzzle of her rifle press firm against the sheriff's throat. "Get on back there," she said.

Sheriff Gibbs's eyes narrowed. Yet what choice did he have? Cherry followed him back to the furthest cell. Checking his pockets to make sure he didn't have a key hidden on him, she pushed him into the cell, slamming the iron door hard behind him.

Reaching up, she took the key to the cell off the hook on the wall and slipped it into her pocket.

"I hope my pa never lets you outta there," she said. Lowering her rifle, she hurried back to the front of the building.

"Help me strip his shirt off, Cherry," Doc

Milton said. "He's hurt bad, and we best hurry." Doc Milton shook his head. "A Texas Ranger. Who'da thought it?"

"My pa," Cherry breathed. She understood—in that moment she understood why her pa had wanted her to stay away from Lobo McCoy.

Arthur Ray had known the moment Lobo had told him his first name that he was a Ranger. It had been Arthur who had revealed Lobo's last name—told Cherry, Mrs. Blakely, and Lefty Pierce not to mention it to the townsfolk. No doubt Arthur suspected Lobo was gunning for Black Jack Haley or some other outlaw. He'd wanted Cherry to stay clean away from the trouble the fact of it might bring. Nobody in the world knew the danger a Texas Ranger's woman faced better than Arthur Ray did—Texas Ranger Arthur Ray, whose young wife had been killed in a shootout between Arthur Ray and a man who'd escaped from prison and come gunning for him.

Cherry had been a baby when her mother had been killed. She didn't remember it, of course, but she had been told the story by her pa once, and she'd read about it in an old paper Mrs. Blakely kept in the trunk in her room.

A murdering outlaw named Parson Shea had escaped from a prison near San Antonio and gone gunning for the Ranger that brought him in—Arthur Ray. Arthur didn't know Parson Shea had escaped and had no reason to suspect he or his wife and new baby girl were in danger. Parson Shea rode into Blue Water. Telling folks he was a cowhand looking for work, he was sent out to Arthur Ray's ranch. He dropped two of Cherry's pa's cowboys before he headed toward the house. Arthur heard the shots and crutched himself out to the lean-to. He'd told his wife, Jenny, to stay inside with the baby—to lay low under the bed in the bedroom. But when Jenny Ray heard the gunfire start, she was frightened—worried for her husband's safety. After all, Arthur had lost a leg in the war and wasn't as healthy and hearty as he once was. Jenny had left the baby safely swaddled under the bed and gone to help her husband. Leveling a rifle at the outlaw, Jenny Ray fired through the kitchen window. Her bullet grazed Parson Shea's head but didn't daze him enough to keep him from shooting back. Arthur Ray dropped Parson Shea cold dead—but not before Parson Shea had triggered, hitting Jenny Ray square in the bosom.

"Let's just tear his shirt off," Doc Milton was saying. "He's too big to strip easy. We can rip through his britches when the time comes."

Cherry brushed tears from her cheeks and laid the rifle on the floor beside Lobo. Quickly, she helped Doc Milton tear Lobo's vest and shirt. A folded length of paper slipped from Lobo's vest pocket as she tossed it out of the way.

Doc Milton shook his head and said, "That'd

most likely be his Warrant of Authority. Gibbs is a dang fool!"

Cherry picked up the paper, shoving it into her pocket with Lobo's badge.

"Help me roll him over," Doc Milton said.

Lobo's lifeless body was heavy and difficult to maneuver. Still, she managed to help Doc Milton roll him over, grimacing as she saw the three bloody holes in Lobo's shoulder and arm.

Again, Doc Milton shook his head. "This here's one tough boy," he mumbled. "Look there," he mumbled, pointing to five scars on Lobo's back. The scars were each about the size of a nickel—visible proof Lobo had survived being shot before. "I wouldn't be surprised to find he's got more the like on him somewhere else. I always sit in wonder at how one man can find himself cold in the ground from one bullet . . . but then some feller like this comes along who seems to be a walkin' miracle."

Cherry brushed the tears from her cheeks. "W-will he be all right this time?"

Doc Milton shook his head, "I don't know. I just don't know."

Cherry winced as Doc Milton stuck his finger into one of the bullet wounds on Lobo's shoulder.

"They ain't deep. I think I can pull 'em all out all right . . . as long as they're all this shallow."

"The men who shot him weren't too awful close to us."

"Good thing. Them bein' so far is probably what saved him this long."

"There's hot water in that kettle on the stove."

"Bring it on over. I'll see to these here shots in his shoulder and arm first off. Then we'll get to the rest."

Cherry looked at the open wounds on Lobo's shoulder and arm. Slowly her gaze traveled over his back to the tear in his britches—the one he'd gotten while jumping the fence to avoid old Snort. The seat of his britches was covered in blood now, as was his leg just below.

Cherry suddenly felt very dizzy. She thought of Lobo's kissing her beneath her mother's cherry tree. She could still taste the sweet flavor of summer cherries in her mouth—still feel his hands in her hair—his strong arms binding her to him. He couldn't die! He couldn't! If Lobo died, Cherry was certain her own heart would quit beating. She'd ask her pa to bury her next to him—so that she could lie with him forever—turn to dust with him close to her.

"Tear his shirt into strips for me, Cherry. I'm gonna dig these bullets out."

Cherry looked to Lobo—studied his face for a moment. How she wished his eyes would open and look at her!

"Come on now, Cherry Ray. You brung him this far. Don't you go faintin' on me now."

"I-I won't," she whispered as she watched Doc

Milton insert some sort of medical tool into one of the wounds at Lobo's shoulder. "I won't."

There was a knock on the jailhouse door, and Billy Parker's voice hollered, "I brung yer pa, Cherry!"

As Doc Milton placed a strip of cloth over the wound at Lobo's leg, Cherry felt suddenly more hopeful knowing her pa had arrived. Leaping to her feet, Cherry drew the bolt and opened the door, collapsing into her pa's strong embrace.

"There now, darlin'," Arthur Ray said.

"They shot him, pa!" she cried. "Just rode out onto our ranch and shot him cold in the back!"

"I know, honey," Arthur said. "I know." He held Cherry away from him, brushed the tears from her cheeks, and asked Doc Milton, "Is he gonna live?"

"I think so. He lost a lot of blood though. He's gonna be too awful weak to be gunnin' for outlaws for a time, I'm afraid."

Cherry watched as Arthur turned to Billy. Bracing himself on one crutch, he said, "You run on home, Bill. But you make sure you do what I said, all right?"

"Yes, sir, Mr. Ray," Billy said. The boy looked to Cherry and frowned. "We all shoulda known it, Cherry—that he was a lawman."

She only nodded and wiped more tears from her cheeks.

"I brung my wagon," Arthur said. "I figure we best take him home with us. Word'll be out soon enough he's a Ranger gunnin' for Black Jack . . . and that won't set well with Jack's boys."

"I agree," Doc Milton said. "I dug out them bullets," he said, nodding to the five bullets lying on the floor next to Lobo. "I think he'll be fine, but ya best move him quick so he can start into healin'."

"There ain't no commotion in town yet," Arthur said.

"Where's the sheriff?" a large red-haired man hollered, bursting into the room. "Where's the sheriff? That outlaw done shot my brother!"

Instantly, Cherry recognized the man as one of the men that had shot Lobo.

"Pa," Cherry breathed. "He—he's one of the ones that shot Lobo."

"That's him! That's him right there!" the man shouted. "And that's the girl that was with him!" The man started to draw his gun but was rendered unconscious as Arthur Ray struck him hard in the head with the butt of his pistol.

Tommy and Miles Baxter stumbled into the room then. They looked to their father, sprawled out on the floor near Lobo.

Arthur Ray leveled his pistol at Tommy's head. "You boys the ones that was bullyin' them kids out on my ranch today?"

"That outlaw done shot our uncle!" Miles said, pointing an index finger to where Lobo lay still unconscious.

"That there's Texas Ranger Lobo McCoy," Arthur said. "And if that other feller on the floor is yer pa, he's in a heap a trouble."

"Lobo McCoy?" Tommy whispered. "Ain't . . . ain't he got a brother?"

"Jefferson McCoy," Miles mumbled. "That Ranger that was gunned down in San Antonio 'fore we left."

"Gunned down by Black Jack Haley," Arthur said. "Lobo's here to bring ol' Jack to justice."

Arthur pushed the barrel of his pistol firm against Tommy Baxter's head. "My name's Arthur Ray—Texas Ranger Arthur Ray—and I'm wantin' to know which one of you boys roughed up them kids today. Which one of you was it that touched my daughter here?"

The still bloodied and bruising Baxter boys stood silent and trembling—terrified in the presence of a man the likes of Arthur Ray.

"Doc," Arthur began, "why don't we stick these boys in a cell 'til I can get back here and deal with them proper."

"You bet," Doc Milton said. Wiping his hands on his shirt, Doc Milton headed to the back of the jailhouse. "Cherry already locked up that coward Gibbs."

"Cherry, help the Doc drag this piece of

horse—help Doc drag this other old boy back there as well," Arthur said.

"Yes, Pa," Cherry said, brushing tears from her cheeks.

"This ain't what I wanted for ya, Cherry," Arthur began. "Fallin' for a lawman—it ain't what I wanted."

"But a good lawman, Pa . . . ain't that the best kinda man there is?" she asked, forcing a smile.

Arthur reached up and brushed a smudge of blood from Cherry's cheek.

"I suppose," he said. He glanced at Lobo. "Jack's boys are ridin' in one at a time, Cherry. Won't be more'n a day or two 'til Jack's back too. We gotta get Lobo home and make sure no one knows we have him—least 'til he's good enough to face Jack proper."

She held her breath and looked to Lobo as he groaned low in his throat.

"See if you can get him up on his own feet long enough to get him in the wagon," Arthur said. "I'm gonna talk to them two boys and that coward Gibbs."

Cherry nodded, noting the way her pa twisted his pistol in his hand. He meant to whip every one of them with the butt of his gun—both Baxter boys and Sheriff Gibbs. He'd see Lobo back to the ranch house and safe before riding back to town to deal with the men in the cells.

Another groan from Lobo and Cherry dropped to her knees beside him.

Stroking his hair, she leaned forward. His eyes opened—narrow slits and only for a moment.

"Lobo? We've got to get ya outta here. We gotta take ya someplace safe."

"That sheriff's a fool," he mumbled. "Jack'll be ridin'—ridin' in any day and I—I gotta . . ."

"We gotta get you up and into the wagon, Lobo . . . before too many folks start millin' around town again."

Lobo winced and lifted his head off the floor. Cherry helped him as he struggled to sit up.

"Ow!" he exclaimed, grimacing. His frown deepened as he looked at Cherry. "Don't cry, darlin'," he breathed, obviously in great pain. "I been shot before."

"Five times at once?" she asked, wiping tears from her cheeks.

"Five times?"

"Doc Milton dug five bullets outta ya," she said, pointing to the bloody bullets on the floor.

Lobo reached out, gathering the bullets into one hand. "Here," he said, holding his hand toward her. "Drop 'em in yer pocket. I wanna put them with the other ones I got."

She frowned as he dropped the bloody bullets into her hand. "Go on," he said. "Don't lose 'em now."

She shook her head, astonished. Dropping

the bullets into the pocket that already held his badge, she stood, taking hold of his arm and helping him to stand. He swore several times and put his hand over the wound at his hip.

"This one hurts worse than the rest of 'em do," he mumbled.

"Let's get you into the wagon. I'll make sure nobody's wanderin' around out there."

Lobo stumbled but braced himself on the edge of the sheriff's desk.

"You best hurry and get me out there, Cherry," he said. "This room's spinnin' like a top."

Cherry opened the jailhouse door and peered out into the street. No one was about—not a soul.

"Come on," she said, draping one of Lobo's heavy arms across her shoulders. "Let's get you in the back of the wagon."

It was a difficult chore. Lobo was weak and struggled to climb into the wagon. Still, somehow Cherry managed to get him in. Easing him gently onto the wagon bed, she helped him lie down under an old quilt her pa had had the foresight to bring along.

Moments later, Arthur Ray climbed into the seat of the wagon and slapped the lines at the backs of the team.

"Stay down, boy . . . Cherry," Arthur said. "I don't want to draw no attention to us."

Cherry stretched out in the wagon bed. She

turned to her side—turned to face Lobo as they traveled.

"Did you help that doc dig them bullets out of me?" Lobo asked. He was lying on his stomach—his warm, brown, pain-filled eyes intent on Cherry's frightened blue ones.

"Yes," she said.

"All five of 'em?" His eyes were narrowing. She knew he would be unconscious again in a matter of moments.

"All five of 'em," she confirmed, smiling at him and brushing the perspiration from his forehead with the back of her hand.

She grinned when he grimaced and swore under his breath.

He was unconscious again, and Cherry let more tears trickle from her eyes. He had to be all right! He had to be! He had to heal up and spit cherry pits with her—drag her home to her pa and tattle on her—hold her in the strength of his arms and kiss her.

"I love you," she whispered. "You'll never know how much."

Brushing the tears from her cheeks, Cherry rolled onto her back. Gazing into the pink sky of early sunset, she tried to erase the memory of the shooting—tried to remember only the blissful moments before, the moments when Lobo McCoy had held her in his arms, thrilled her with delicious, cherry-flavored kisses.

CHAPTER ELEVEN

"Shot him square in the back without a hint of a warnin'," Arthur Ray told Lefty Pierce. "Way I heard it, Lobo was up north trailin' some other outlaw when Black Jack and his boys rode into San Antonio. Jack shot Jefferson McCoy and them two deputies."

Lefty shook his head. "So Lobo rode into Blue Water to bring Jack in."

"I shouldn'ta let it go so long," Arthur said. "I know how scared folks are 'round here—how they think the worst of any stranger that rides in, instead of the best. Still, I could tell Lobo didn't want folks a-knowin' he was a Ranger."

"He wanted ol' Jack to ride on into town thinkin' Lobo was plannin' on joinin' up with him and his boys," Lefty said.

"That's right—but I shoulda said somethin', at least to that fool Clarence Gibbs. I'm lucky Lobo and Cherry ain't both lyin' out in the boneyard east of town."

"Well, whether them Baxters knew Lobo was a Ranger or not . . . they still went gunnin'."

"And Clarence Gibbs set 'em out to do it. As far as I'm concerned, Clarence can rot away in them cells with them Baxter fellers even if it takes a week for the law to get here from San Antonio."

"It's a good thing ya brung him here," Lefty said. "Jack's boys woulda finished him off if you'da left him in town to heal."

"Do ya think they know he's here?" Mrs. Blakely asked. "Could be they'll come for him if they do."

"They're too afraid of Pa, even if they do know he's here," Cherry said.

"Well, I hope so . . . but I ain't certain," Arthur said. "I wouldn't have our boys ridin' back and forth all day keepin' watch if I was certain."

"Naw, they won't buck Arthur none," Lefty said. "Not without Jack anyway."

Cherry had tried to sit still—tried to keep herself from Lobo's bedside—but she'd tried long enough.

Rising from the parlor chair she'd been sitting in for the last hour, she said, "I'll go peek in on him . . . just see if he needs anythin'."

"He needs his rest, Cherry," Mrs. Blakely said. "He's never gonna heal if ya don't leave him be."

Cherry frowned and looked to her pa for support. She had to be with Lobo! Certainly she'd sat up with him through the first night, changed his bandages, given him water when he was conscious enough to drink it. Still, Mrs. Blakely had sat with him the second night—after Cherry's pa insisted she needed her rest as well.

"Oh, he oughta be doin' fine by now, Fiona," Arthur said. "None of them bullets hit bone. If he's the ol' wolf I think he is, he'll be fightin' us to get outta bed by noon today. It won't do no harm to let Cherry look in on him for a while this mornin'. Might even lift his spirits."

Mrs. Blakely raised a suspicious eyebrow. "Lift his spirits, indeed," she mumbled. "And speakin' of old wolves," she continued, "I just can't get use to that thing over by the hearth, Cherry. Can't ya take it out to the barn or somethin'?"

Cherry looked to the old dried-up red wolf still curled up in restfulness by the hearth.

"He's fine where he is, Mrs. Blakely," Cherry said. "Look how peaceful and comfortable he is."

"Peaceful?" Mrs. Blakely exclaimed. "Comfortable? He's dead, Cherry Ray! He's up chasin' rabbits in heaven." With an exasperated sigh, Mrs. Blakely turned and stormed toward the kitchen, all the while muttering complaints under her breath.

"Go on in there and see if Lobo's got everythin' he needs," Arthur said. "Let him know I got his horse out in the barn . . . his riggin' too."

"Thanks, Pa."

Hurrying to the spare bedroom where Lobo had been convalescing since being shot, Cherry opened the door quietly. He was sleeping. His eyes were closed and his broad chest rose and fell with the slow rhythm of slumber.

She smiled and entered the room, quietly closing the door behind her. She was almost glad to find him asleep; it meant she could study him without him knowing.

Carefully, she sat down in the chair at the side of the bed, hoping the soft rustle of her petticoats hadn't disturbed him. He'd rolled onto his back, and Cherry winced, wondering if the weight of his body on his wounds against the mattress would cause them to start bleeding again.

Oh, how wonderful he was! Cherry bit her lip, delighted at having another opportunity to stare at him for as long as her heart desired. He was ever so handsome, especially with his hair tousled the way it was. It gave him a rather relaxed appearance. His shoulders and chest were so broad—so perfectly formed and so muscular. Cherry shook her head at the three round scars visible on his left shoulder. Her eyes filled with moisture. Merely from the waist up, it was apparent Lobo had taken at least seven other bullets—seven more than the five he'd taken the day Mr. Baxter and his brother had tried to gun him down under the cherry tree. Even Cherry's pa had been astounded by the amount of bullet wounds visible on Lobo's torso.

Cherry brushed the tears from her cheeks and thought, You have to give this up! You can't go on bein' shot at without a bullet findin' your heart one day!

Shaking her head to dispel the frightening thoughts, she continued to study him. She would never tire of looking at Lobo McCoy. Never!

"If ya think I didn't hear ya come in . . . yer wrong," he mumbled unexpectedly. Cherry's heart began to hammer in her bosom! She was so delighted by the sound of his voice, the warm brown of his eyes as they opened and looked at her, that she thought she might never draw another calm breath in her life.

"H-how are ya feelin'?" she asked. The color had returned to his face, and even though he grimaced when he bent his arm and fisted his hand to test his strength, she could tell he was mending.

"Stiff as a wagon board," he said, frowning as he clutched his right shoulder with his left hand and continued to move his stretch. "I don't know why, but it always seems to take me a day or two to get to movin' around good after I been shot."

Cherry felt her eyebrows arch in disbelief. Was he joshing? Surely he was.

"You were shot five times, Lobo. I'm sure it will take a while before you'll be up and around again."

But Lobo shook his head. "Can't take no longer than it already has," he said. "Black Jack will be ridin' in any day, and I gotta bring him in. He's goin' back to San Antonio to stand before a judge." Lobo tried to sit up but grimaced and let his head fall back against the pillow. "Give me a minute or two . . . then I'll be up."

"You ain't gettin' up in a minute or an hour!" Cherry scolded. "You'll stay right there and rest."

"Where's my gun?" he asked, looking over at her frowning. "Did you have it?"

"It's under the bed," Cherry began, "But ya don't need it just now."

"Hand it up here to me, would ya?" he asked. "I'll sleep better holdin' it in my hand than I will knowin' it's so far away as under the bed."

"I don't think you—"

"Please, Cherry," he interrupted. He looked worried, tired—plum worn out—and she couldn't refuse him.

Shaking her head, she reached under the bed and retrieved Lobo's gun belt, holster, and Colt. She pulled the gun out of the holster, laying the belt and holster on the bed at Lobo's side as she studied the gun.

"Peacemaker," she mumbled, reading aloud the engraving on the brass plate of the gun grip. Her eyes narrowed as she saw the markings carved into the grip. "Twenty-five," she breathed in a whisper. It was true then—what she'd overheard Remmy Cooper and Mr. Murphy saying the day she'd hidden in the barrel.

"That's right," Lobo said, holding his hand out to her in a gesture she should give the weapon to him.

"You've killed twenty-five men?" She'd never heard of a Texas Ranger notching his pistol.

"Nope," he said as she handed the pistol to him. "This ain't my gun. It was Juan Gutierrez claimed he notched it. My brother . . ." He paused and looked at her, deep pain evident in his eyes. "I'm guessin' yer pa's already told you my brother Jefferson was gunned down by Black Jack in San Antonio." Cherry nodded and felt renewed moisture gathering in her eyes.

Lobo frowned and studied the pistol in his hand. "Anyway," he continued, "there was this feller—an outlaw come up to Texas from Mexico, Juan Gutierrez—and he was a bad one. Killed hisself three Texas Rangers, four sheriffs, five deputies, six or seven farmers, and one or two ranchers . . . and that's just the ones we know fer sure. Well, Jefferson and me were trackin' him after he'd gone loco in a saloon over down in Buffalo Gap—gunned down a couple a gamblers and two saloon girls. One of his stray bullets hit a little girl out in the street, and she died too. So Jefferson and me, we tracked old Juan down, but for some reason . . . he just didn't wanna hang."

Cherry smiled when he grinned at her and added, "Though I can't imagine why not."

His eyes narrowed as he studied the gun again. "We had him held up in a dry creek bed outside of San Antonio and were gonna just wait him out . . . figurin' we had more supplies between the two of us than he'd managed to haul away from Buffalo Gap when he run. Well, we was waitin' him out when this other feller, Pepe Ortiz—he rode with Juan sometimes—this Pepe Ortiz comes outta nowhere and shoots me twice in the back. Jefferson shot Pepe, and knowin' I needed to get back to town—bein' that I was bleedin' all over his favorite shirt I'd borrowed the mornin' before—Jefferson just called out to ol' Juan and told him if he didn't give hisself over to us, he'd wake up sproutin' maggots. Ol' Juan thought, with me wounded, he'd take Jefferson down easy. But it wasn't so. Juan come runnin' at Jefferson, and Jefferson's hollerin' at him to stop or he'll drop him. So Juan stops cold and so did Jefferson. They eyed each other up a bit . . . but Jefferson was a quicker draw than Juan and shot that mean ol' outlaw right between the eyes."

Cherry hadn't realized her mouth had dropped open as she'd been drawn into Lobo's story. When she did, she closed it and swallowed the lump in her throat. It was all too clear in her mind—the danger he'd been in—his being shot.

"Here, see there?" Lobo said, turning the gun over and pointing to the brass plate on the other side of the grip. "Taylor Aimes," he read. Cherry hadn't noticed the engraving on the opposite side of the grip of the one reading Peacemaker; she hadn't noticed it read differently. "Texas Ranger," Lobo read. "He was one of the Rangers Juan had gunned down. Jefferson took Juan's gun—said it needed to be used fer good the way Aimes had meant it to be. He carried it from then on. I think he thought if he could drop twenty-five outlaws with it, it might make ol' Aimes rest easier."

"So . . . so now you carry it," Cherry said.

Lobo nodded. "Yep. I got my own gun, of course. It's a might purtier than this one—has my name engraved on it too," he said, grinning. He shook his head and added, "But I decided I'd carry this one. As long as Black Jack Haley's free to murder, I'll carry this one. If it was good enough fer Jefferson, then I figure it's good enough for me." His frown deepened, and Cherry saw the moisture gathering in his eyes. "I can't lay here feelin' sorry for myself much longer, Cherry," he said. "I gotta bring Jack in. You understand?"

"Yes," Cherry whispered. She did. Yet the selfish part of her—the part that wanted to own Lobo's heart—the selfish part of her wanted him to forget about bringing Black Jack Haley to justice.

"It's why I came here," he said. "It's why I've been waitin' around, bidin' my time 'til Jack gets comfortable and rides back into Blue Water. It's a good reason . . . don't ya think?"

Cherry nodded. "B-but when it's over . . . when you've got him, taken him back to San Antonio . . . what then?"

She watched as Lobo's eyes lingered on her. "I ride a dangerous trail, Cherry. Yer pa knows it."

"Pa rode that same trail once . . . but not anymore."

He grinned at her, chuckled, and said, "What do ya want me to do, Sweet Cherry Ray? Toss my badge in the river and spend the rest of my days swappin' cherry pits with you?"

Cherry felt herself blushing, felt overly warm, humiliated somehow. Yet mustering all the courage she could in that moment, she asked, "What would be so terrible about that?"

Lobo's smile faded. She felt uncomfortable under his piercing gaze.

"Fact is," he began, "I can't think of anythin' I'd like better."

Cherry dared to look at him—half expecting a teasing smile to be on his lips—but he wasn't smiling.

"But you don't know me, Cherry," he said. "How can ya? I've only been in Blue Water a couple a weeks. Hell, half the time you've been with me, I've been tattlin' on ya to yer pa." His eyes narrowed then as he added, "And the other half I been slobberin' all over ya like a wet pup."

"If . . . if I looked more like Pinky Chitter and less like I oughta be my own brother—" Cherry began.

"Well, that's just about the dumbest thing I ever heard come outta yer mouth, girl!" he growled. He frowned and wagged an index finger at her as he asked, "You wanna know the last time I was so distracted by a woman, Cherry?"

Cherry frowned, not wanting to know—not wanting to hear about other women he had known. She shook her head, but he answered anyway.

"I was sixteen, and the schoolmarm was eighteen. She backed me in a corner after school one day and kissed me the like I had never imagined. That was it! I was plum gone on her . . . though she wasn't as plum gone on me. But I couldn't think straight to save my life! I was always headin' into trouble, making a dang fool of myself. She married the sheriff in our town when I was eighteen . . . dropped me like a hot potata. That's when I decided to ranger with Jefferson."

Cherry tried to remain calm, but her body was trembling. She needed escape—escape or to be in his arms! One or the other.

"Ain't a woman I courted or been involved with since that got me that frustrated, confused, and just plain wound up," he said. He looked angry. "Nope, notta one . . . that is, 'til I come ridin' into Blue Water one day with revenge on my mind and find some purty little thing dressed up in boys' britches and standin' in the street with a dried-up ol' wolf at her feet."

Cherry watched, overwhelmed with emotion as Lobo struggled to right himself. Sitting up, he swung his legs over the side of the bed and reached out, taking hold of the bodice of her dress.

"How'd yer ma die, Cherry?" Lobo asked, his eyes burning with frustration and anger. Cherry swallowed and tried to force the tears in her eyes to stay steady—tried to keep them from escaping over her cheeks. "How'd she die?"

"Sh-she was shot."

"That's right," Lobo growled. "By an old outlaw gunnin' fer yer pa. Fuss Ingram told me the story when I was playin' cards with him the other day." Cherry's tears escaped and trickled over her cheeks as he spoke to her.

"S-so yer a coward?" she asked. "That's what's keepin' ya from—"

"I ain't no coward, Cherry," he said. "But I ain't no fool neither. I won't see you hurt because of me. Out there the other day, under that cherry tree—one more minute, one straighter shot, and you mighta been dead because of someone gunnin' for me."

"They were gunnin' for ya because ya beat their boys, not because yer a Ranger . . . and ya wouldn't have had to beat their boys if it wasn't for me."

"Black Jack will be ridin' in soon," Lobo said, perspiration gathering on his forehead. "And when he does, someone'll tell him there's a Texas Ranger lookin' for him, and then he will be gunnin' for me."

"So shoot him first and stay here with me," Cherry breathed as tears trickled down her face.

Lobo grimaced, as if the sight of her tears were more painful than the five bullet holes in his back.

"Cherry!" Mrs. Blakely exclaimed in a whisper as she burst into the room.

Cherry let her eyes plead with Lobo's for a moment, but he looked away and let go of the front of her dress.

She brushed the tears from her cheeks and turned to face Mrs. Blakely.

"What is it?" she asked. She was unsettled as she looked to the old woman to see her face void of color, her hands wringing.

"Griff saw Fuss Ingram," Mrs. Blakely said. "He's ridin' this way with Tucker Johnson and Lee Taylor."

"Where're my britches?" Lobo growled, trying to stand.

"Arthur says yer to stay put, Mr. McCoy," Mrs. Blakely said.

"Like hell I will!" Lobo growled, trying to stand again. "Get me my britches, or I'll face him in my underwear if I have to."

"Yer pa says not to let him out of this room, Cherry," Mrs. Blakely said.

"What?" Lobo hollered. "I'll go where I want to, and when!"

"Hush, Mr. McCoy!" Mrs. Blakely scolded.

"They're ridin' up to the house right this minute. Arthur says he'll send 'em back to town. They won't do much without Jack with 'em."

"Settle on down, Lobo," Cherry said, taking hold of his arms as he managed to get to his feet. "Let pa take care of it . . . for now."

"I won't sit here like a scared pup and let yer pa get hisself killed!" Lobo shouted. Perspiration beaded on his chest and face. He was in great pain and in no condition to face outlaws.

"I'll lock the door and make some noise in case he don't quit fussin'," Mrs. Blakely said. Cherry nodded as Mrs. Blakely left the room. She heard the key turn in the lock on the other side of the door.

"You let me outta here, Cherry!" Lobo hollered.

"Hush! They'll hear you!"

"I . . . I want 'em to hear me!" he panted. "I ain't gonna hide in here . . . hide behind yer pa's gun! Yer pa did his job. He don't hafta do it no more!"

Awkwardly—for it was apparent he was in great pain—Lobo reached back, picking his gun and belt up off the bed.

"You put that gun down, Lobo McCoy!"

"Keep him quiet, Cherry!" Mrs. Blakely exclaimed from the other side of the door.

"I'm tryin'!" she exclaimed in return. Panic washed over her! If Fuss Ingram and the others found Lobo in such a weakened condition, they'd kill him for certain.

"Well, try harder!"

"You go on and move outta my way, Cherry," Lobo said, limping toward her, hooking his gun belt over his left shoulder.

Cherry shook her head, relieved when she heard Mrs. Blakely's familiar, if not terrible, piano playing drifting from the parlor.

"Beautiful dreamer, wake unto me . . ." Mrs. Blakely's rather sour voice began to sing.

Lobo scowled. "She sounds awful!" he growled.

"Keep quiet, Lobo. Let pa take care of it this time."

"They'll shoot yer pa, Cherry," he said. "I can't let that—"

"Stay here with me," she said, placing her palms on his chest. Gazing into the warm brown of his pain-filled eyes, she pleaded, "Let pa take care of it . . . just today. Black Jack ain't with them, and none of them have the courage to go against pa. Wait a few days . . . 'til yer strength is back. Just—just stay here with me for now."

"Lulled by the moonlight have all passed away," Mrs. Blakely's vinegary voice sang. Lobo grimaced again.

"Cherry," he said, swaying slightly. "I can't let yer pa—"

"Just sit down and let it pass, Lobo," she said, gently pushing him back toward the bed.

"If I go," he began, "they won't kill yer pa."

"They won't kill him."

"They'll kill one of us if they get the chance. Better me than yer pa, don't ya think?"

Cherry felt the tears leave her eyes, felt guilt pinch her heart, desperation grip her soul. "No," she whispered. She couldn't let him go! Not for any reason—not even for her pa's sake. Furthermore, she knew her pa would understand—that her pa would've made the same decision were the choice his own.

Lobo frowned—sat down hard on the bed as if he'd been slapped to sudden consciousness.

"Stay here with me, Lobo," Cherry whispered, as his hands went to her waist. "For now . . . for now just stay here with me . . . just for a few more minutes . . . just 'til they're gone."

Lobo's fevered mind fought for understanding—truth. Surely she hadn't just told him she'd choose his life over her daddy's? Surely not! She'd only said it to stun him—to keep him too confused to break out of the room. The tears on her beautiful cheeks and what he saw in her eyes, however, told him differently.

He tried to think of his murdered brother, of the pain his body was experiencing because of his wounds. He tried to think of Black Jack Haley, of Pepe Ortiz—anything that might distract him from the beautiful young woman standing before him now. She was right; he was too weak to face anybody, let alone three healthy outlaws. The fever he felt, the pain, the weakness in his limbs—he might not survive if he faced Fuss Ingram and the others in that moment. And suddenly—suddenly he wanted to survive! Suddenly, Lobo McCoy wanted something besides justice and revenge. Suddenly the only thing Lobo McCoy cared about was the only thing he'd ever wanted so badly he was willing to sacrifice his pride, strength, and life for. Suddenly, the only thing Lobo McCoy wanted was Cherry Ray.

"I-I have to bring Jack in," Lobo stammered.

"You will," Cherry said, reaching out and running her fingers through his already tousled hair. "But when yer able. If ya go out to face his boys now..."

"I-I have to leave once I get him," Lobo mumbled.

Cherry was relieved he'd finally lowered his voice—hoped Mrs. Blakely would stop singing, quit causing Stephen Foster to roll over in his grave.

"Just stay simmered down for a few more—" Cherry began.

Lobo suddenly reached up, gathering the fabric of her dress bodice in his fists. Cherry gasped, delighted as he pulled her to him, their mouths meeting—the fiery passion blazing between them instant and all-consuming.

"Afternoon, Arthur," Fuss Ingram said.

Arthur Ray stood, rifle leveled, Lefty Pierce behind him. He wished Fiona would stop that dang cat-screeching!

"Fuss . . . Tucker . . . Lee," Arthur greeted. "What're you boys doin' out so far from town?"

Fuss's eyes narrowed. "Well, Arthur," he began, "fact is, we heard that new stranger in town is actually Lobo McCoy . . . a purty famous Texas Ranger outta San Antonio."

"Ain't that interestin'?" Arthur said. "But I still don't know why you boys are out my way."

"Well," Fuss began, "we figure you Rangers are thicker'n sap and that ya might be hidin' him out here. Word in town is he got in a tangle with a couple a red-haired boys and ended up shot in the back."

"Only a fool coward would shoot Lobo McCoy in the back and let him live to come gunnin' for him," Arthur said. "Besides, what do you boys care if he did get hisself shot? He ain't caused ya no trouble, has he?"

Fuss looked to Tucker, to Lee, and then back to Arthur. "Well, no, he ain't. But we figure he's here gunnin' for Jack . . . and I'm sure Jack would rather we take care of the problem 'fore he gets back and has to take care of it hisself."

Arthur chuckled and nodded. "Oh, that's right," he said. "I always forget you boys is just pups still hangin' on the teat. It's a wonder Jack had the guts to shoot that Ranger in the back in San Antonio. With you boys around . . . seems to me he don't usually hafta have the guts."

"Now we don't want no trouble, Arthur," Tucker said. The outlaw stepped back a ways as Arthur raised the level of his gun barrel.

"Then ya oughta just hurry on back to town for a game a cards," Arthur said. "If'n that was my brother you all shot in San Antonio, I'da dropped everyone of ya cold already."

"Is he with ya, Arthur?" Fuss asked.

"Do you see him with me?"

"Ol' Jack won't be happy if he finds out you been hidin' that Ranger," Fuss said.

"And I'm sure ol' Jack won't be happy if he rides into Blue Water to find yer ugly carcasses hangin' from a tree neither."

Fuss straightened his shoulders at the threat, but Arthur kept on. "Hell's comin' fer Jack, boys. One way or the other, it's comin' for him. You wanna go down with him, that's yer choice. But goin' down without him is plum foolish. And believe me, tryin' to back a wounded wolf into a corner the way yer doin' is one sure way of gettin' yerself killed. Now you go on and tell me Jack's worth all that, and I'll tell you right where that wounded wolf is."

The men were quiet, obviously considering what Arthur Ray had said.

"Best wait 'til Jack gets back, Fuss," Tucker said.

"Yeah," Lee added. "After all, Jack might want another Texas Ranger notch on his own pistol."

Fuss's eyes narrowed. "Maybe he wants two."

"Maybe," Arthur said.

Fuss exhaled an angry sigh. "Well then . . . I guess we'll be seein' ya in town, Arthur."

"I guess."

Arthur watched the three outlaws mount and ride off before he closed the door.

"Fer Pete's sake, Fiona!" he exclaimed. "You know I can't stand Stephen Foster!"

Cherry reveled in the feel of Lobo's unshaven face between her hands—the delicious flavor of his kiss! Even for his weakened condition, he sent her heart to hammering—goose bumps breaking over her arms and legs. She loved the scent of his skin, the fevered heat of his mouth as he demanded she allow his marvelous affections.

He swayed slightly, and she knew he was weak—dizzy because of his wounds.

Breaking the seal of their lips, Cherry held Lobo's face between her hands, gazing into the warm brown of his eyes.

"They're gone," she whispered. "They're gone, and you need to rest."

"I need you," he mumbled, kissing her again.

It was sheer fear—fear for his well-being that enabled Cherry to break from him once more.

"Lay down," she said, gently pushing at his chest. He closed his eyes, and she helped him to lie back down in the bed.

"Yer pa's gonna shoot me when he finds out I been kissin' . . . that I been kissin' his daughter right under his own roof . . . and in my underwear, to boot," Lobo mumbled.

"Just rest," Cherry told him, smoothing the wrinkle in his brow.

"What'd ya do with that ol' wolf, anyhow, Cherry Ray? Did ya keep it or throw it in the fire somewhere?"

Cherry smiled. Lobos were a breed of timber wolf. She'd never thought of it before—the fact she'd drug Ol' Red home the very day Lobo had ridden into Blue Water.

"I kept it," she said, laying one hand against his fevered cheek. "I'll always keep it."

CHAPTER TWELVE

Arthur Ray studied the young man sitting across from him on the porch. Lobo McCoy was a fine man—a fine man and a fine Texas Ranger. He was strong too. It hadn't even been a whole week since Lobo had taken five bullets in the back. And yet there he sat, looking as healthy as a horse and strong as an ox. Yep—Arthur Ray had never known a man good enough for his daughter—until now.

"You given any more thought to what we talked about the other day at the boardin' house?" Arthur asked.

Lobo's eyebrows arched—his attention still fixed on the stick he was whittling with the knife he'd pulled from his boot a few minutes before.

"Ya mean about ridin' a different trail?"

"That's the one." Oh, he knew by the way the boy wouldn't look at him that he'd given it more thought than he had almost anything else over the past few days.

Lobo stopped whittling and looked to Arthur. His eyes narrowed. "She's why you let Jack linger in town without no trouble for so long, ain't she?" he asked. "You were afraid that if ya tried to bring him in and he dropped ya cold . . . then Cherry would be left all alone."

Arthur didn't answer with words—only nodded.

"I wondered why Texas Ranger Arthur Ray would allow an outlaw to go unpunished."

"When did ya figure it?"

Lobo shrugged. "I guess the day I caught her spyin' on me in the creek and drug her on back here. The minute I figured who you were."

"Are ya thinkin' I'm a coward?"

Lobo frowned and shook his head. "No, sir! Ain't many men who could swallow their pride . . . let a thing like that go for the sake of their girl. Especially one who'd spent most of his life bringin' men like Black Jack Haley to the hangman's noose."

"But then you come along," Arthur said.

Lobo nodded. "That's right. I come along. And I'll take care of Jack for you, sir . . . for both of us."

"You'll take care of Cherry for both of us."

Lobo frowned.

"What?"

"You think I'm gonna let you go after Jack when Cherry feels the way she does about you?" Arthur shook his head. "No, sir! I ain't gonna let her stand there and see you get gunned down—watch her heart and spirit break—know she'll never smile again. Nope. You come here for a reason, Lobo. You were brung here . . . brung here to take care of my Sweet Cherry so I could finally face down ol' Jack."

"Now hang on there—" Lobo began.

"I know you think I'm old," Arthur interrupted. "And havin' only one leg left slows me down some . . . but I can still drop Jack 'fore he clears leather."

Lobo paused for a moment. Arthur knew the boy's thoughts were wrestling with each other. He lowered his voice, wagging the knife in his hand at Arthur as he spoke.

"I ain't been here a month, Mr. Ray. She don't even know me. And she sure as hell wouldn't want to watch you die before she would me."

Arthur smiled. "Cherry's been lovin' on you since the day you rode in, Lobo. The trail's partin' . . . and I ain't stupid. Yer already reinin' over to this here new trail . . . and I ain't gonna let ya go back."

"Jefferson would want me to—"

"I think it's yer brother would want you to be happy—to know yer loved by Cherry and lovin' her in return," Arthur said. "He don't want you up in heaven with him yet. He's got plenty a dead Rangers up there to saddle around with for now."

Lobo sighed and hung his head. The pain of losing his brother was still fresh in him.

Arthur sighed and added, "It helps me to think of 'em all that way . . . all them dead Texas Rangers I knew. It helps me to think of 'em up there, sittin' 'round a fire talkin', their ponies tied up for the night. Maybe somebody's got his harmonica out, a-playin' a tune." He looked to Lobo, his eyes narrowing. "Yer brother's probably with 'em. And do ya really think any one of 'em would rather see ya joinin' in with 'em up there rather than havin' Cherry fer yer own right here?"

"She sure gets me to twistin' every dang direction," Lobo mumbled. "I can't hardly think of nothin' else at all these days."

"Then don't," Arthur said.

Lobo shook his head. "I keep thinkin' about Cherry's mama though."

"Everybody you ever brought in hanged. Ain't that right?"

Lobo smiled. "Yep. Unless they was dead already."

"Then you ain't got nothin' to worry about when it comes to somethin' happening to Cherry."

"Except for Jack and his boys."

Arthur nodded. "I'll take care of Jack and his boys."

"You givin' me permission to court Cherry then, Mr. Ray?"

Arthur smiled. He liked the boy's humility.

"I'm givin' you permission to do far more'n that, Lobo McCoy." Arthur chuckled as Lobo smiled. "Now, I'm wantin' at least five or six grandchildren outta this here deal."

Lobo reached out and patted Arthur's knee. "I'll get to it right away, Mr. Ray," he began, "soon as I bring ol' Jack back to San Antonio for ya."

"I'll bring ol' Jack in, Lobo. Yer just gonna stay here and marry Cherry."

"Now, don't you be—"

"What are you two up to out here?" Cherry said as she opened the front door and stepped out onto the porch.

Arthur looked to Lobo, who dropped his gaze and started whittling on the stick again.

"Just passin' the time, honey," Cherry's pa said.

Cherry smiled. It was such a sweet, rather calming vision—her pa and Lobo sitting there in Mrs. Blakely's old rockers just wasting the day away. It had been a long time since she'd seen her pa look so—so content. She wondered at it. Knowing that Black Jack would ride back into Blue Water and come gunning for Lobo, how could they both sit there so relaxed, seeming so carefree?

Cherry felt the hair prickle at the back of her neck—fear and worry over Lobo's health and safety. At the same time, he looked up at her and winked, sending goose bumps racing over her arms.

"Well, Mrs. Blakely says it's nearly time for lunch and that the two of you should get washed up," Cherry said. She tried to force another smile—tried to appear as if she wasn't dithering between intense fear and worry over Lobo's safety and well-being and delight at having had so much time in his company over the past few days.

"I don't need to wash up," Arthur grumbled. "I ain't done a dang thing all day."

"I know, Pa . . . but you know how particular she is about—"

Cherry looked up when she heard Billy's voice. Her pa looked too, and Lobo stood up from his chair.

"Mr. Ray! Mr. Ray!" Billy called.

Cherry shaded her eyes from the sun. Griff was riding up to the ranch house hard and fast, with Billy Parker sitting in the saddle behind him.

"What's all this, Griff?" Arthur asked the cowboy.

"Found the boy runnin' hell-bent for the ranch, Mr. Ray. Says ol' Jack's back in Blue Water and—"

"He shot Pinky Chitter, Mr. Ray!" Billy said, hopping down off the horse and running up the front porch steps. "He shot her square in the chest! She's dead, Mr. Ray! Black Jack shot Pinky cold dead—not an hour ago—right there in the saloon!"

"What?" Cherry gasped. "But . . . but she's his girl!" she breathed.

"Why'd he go and shoot her, boy?" Arthur

asked. "He's been hangin' onto Pinky near to five years. What went on?"

Billy bent over, placing his hands on his knees as he tried to catch his breath.

"He . . . he . . . well, the way I heard it from Remmy Cooper . . . Jack said Pinky didn't tell him the truth about Lobo McCoy! Jack said Pinky knew Lobo was a Ranger and that she saw him get in the wagon with Cherry the day he was shot. Pinky was lookin' out the saloon window when Doc Milton went into the jailhouse . . . and when I brung you in, Mr. Ray. She was still watchin' when Cherry put Lobo in the wagon . . . way Remmy tells it anyway. Jack was mad that Pinky didn't tell his boys that she knew fer sure you was hidin' Lobo here, Mr. Ray. Jack said that if she'd told Fuss the truth, Fuss, Lee, and Tucker coulda taken care of Lobo 'fore Jack ever got back . . . but since she didn't tell them, they didn't go up against you to get to Lobo. Jack was mad about it . . . mad that his boys didn't take care of Lobo when he was laid up. So he shot Pinky Chitter for it—just drew his iron and shot her! And now . . . now he's gunnin' for Lobo . . . says he's gonna drop that purty Ranger dead cold next to Pinky."

Cherry felt tears trickling over her cheeks. Pinky Chitter—dead? She couldn't believe it! After all those years of being loyal to Black Jack—how could he kill her so heartlessly?

Lobo slipped the knife he'd been using to whittle back into his boot.

"He's turnin' on the town, Mr. Ray," Lobo said. "If he's willin' to shoot her so easy—"

"I know. Ain't nobody in Blue Water safe no more."

Lobo's hand rested on the grip of his pistol for a moment.

"I can't let this go no longer, Mr. Ray," he began, "You know I can't let this go."

"I can't let it go neither," Arthur said. "In a way, this is my fault, and I need to answer for it." Arthur shook his head. "Miss Pinky Chitter. I can't hardly believe it."

Lobo turned to Cherry—took her shoulders between strong hands.

"It's what I came here for, Cherry," he said. "I gotta finish it. I gotta finish it for Jefferson, for myself . . . for everyone in Blue Water. But mostly, I gotta finish it for you. If I don't finish this . . . I hafta finish it, or I can't have you."

Cherry was certain her heart stopped! Her breathing certainly had!

"What?" she whispered.

"I'll take care of Jack . . . haul him back to San Antonio," Lobo said. "Then I'll ride on back here and toss my badge in some old trunk for our grandkids to find someday and spend the rest of my life swappin' cherry pits with you." He frowned—a fearful, worried expression puckering his brow. "If—if you'll marry me, that is."

"Y-yer teasin' me," Cherry whispered. Surely it couldn't be! Surely Lobo McCoy—famous Texas Ranger, handsomest man in the whole of Texas—surely he wasn't proposing marriage to her—to silly little Sweet Cherry Ray?

She watched as Lobo's warm brown eyes narrowed, as the alluring smile she loved so much spread across his handsome face.

"Will you marry me?" He took her face between his strong hands and kissed her square on the mouth—before her pa and Billy and the whole wide world! "If I take the different trail and give up rangerin' . . . will you marry me, Sweet Cherry Ray?"

"Yes!" Billy Parker exclaimed. "Of course she will!"

Cherry smiled—reveled in the feel of Lobo's thumbs gently brushing the tears from her cheeks.

"Of course," Cherry breathed. "I'll marry you no matter what ya do—Texas Ranger or not. I love you and I'll marry you! The very moment this is over! I promise!"

Lobo's smile broadened. "Then let me finish this . . . for you, for yer pa, for me, and for my brother." He kissed her again—fierce, moist, and warm—and Cherry thought her heart would burst from owning so much joy.

"We already talked this out, boy," Arthur said

as he crutched down the steps. "I'm the one who let Jack run this town fer so long. I'll take care of him now."

"He's turned, Mr. Ray," Lobo said. "If he's willin' to kill Pinky, he'll drop anybody dead . . . especially the only man he's been afraid of all these years."

"I ain't gonna stand by and see you killed," Arthur said.

Lobo looked to Cherry. She was so beautiful! In that brief moment, he noticed the sunlight caressing her hair, the blue of her dress reflected in her eyes. His mouth watered—every inch of his body longed to hold her—to kiss her. He saw something else in her expression—fear and compassion—fear for his safety and compassion for her daddy's pride. He knew who she could not bear to lose. If Black Jack was going to drop a Texas Ranger, Lobo's heart told him that even for her guilt and self-hatred, she could not lose him. Still, he would not let her lose her daddy either. Nor would he let her daddy's pride suffer. Arthur Ray was perhaps the greatest lawman to ever ride out in Texas, and he needed to see Black Jack brought to justice. Furthermore, he needed to have a hand in it.

Lobo's heart hammered in his chest. There was a fork in the trail before him . . . and he would not let anyone take his chance at happiness from him—especially Black Jack Haley. He'd ride to town with Arthur, and they'd bring him in—alive or dead. They'd bring him in and free Blue Water—free themselves.

"Then we'll take him together," Lobo said, offering a hand to Arthur.

"Let's ride."

"I'm comin' with you," Cherry said, hurrying down the steps.

"You'll stay here," Lobo growled, taking hold of her arm. "I don't need no distractions. If he shot Pinky so easy, he'll shoot anybody just the same."

"But I can't stay here!"

"You stay here where it's safe," Arthur commanded. "Keep the boy here too." Arthur turned to Billy and added, "You stay away from town 'til one of us rides back with it all bein' over."

"But my ma will be worried," Billy said.

"I'll let yer ma know yer all right." Arthur patted the young man on the shoulder with reassurance.

"You can't leave me here!" Cherry exclaimed. "I can't just sit here and wait like this! I can't!"

"What's goin' on out here?" Mrs. Blakely grumbled, stepping from the house onto the front porch.

"Black Jack killed Pinky Chitter, Mrs. Blakely!" Billy answered.

"Please, Lobo," Cherry pleaded, taking hold of his arm. "You can't just expect me to—"

Lobo gathered her into his arms. Oh, how she loved being held by him—loved the scent of soap and leather about him.

"Please, Cherry," he mumbled into her hair. "I won't be able to concentrate on Black Jack unless I know yer safe. Please . . . if you want me as bad as I want you, you'll stay here . . . so I'll know you'll be waitin' for me when we're finished with Jack and his boys."

"B-but you're still hurt," Cherry sobbed.

"I'm well enough."

"Let's go," Arthur mumbled, moving past the others toward the barn. "Help me saddle my pony, would ya, Griff?"

"Yes, sir, Mr. Ray."

"Come on, Lobo. Let's get this over with."

Lobo kissed Cherry hard on the mouth, causing Mrs. Blakely to gasp and tisk her tongue with disapproval.

"I love you, Cherry Ray. Since the minute I saw you with that danged ol' dried-up wolf."

Cherry let the tears flow bountifully over her cheeks. "I love you," she whispered. "Come back to me. Promise you'll come back to me."

"I promise," he said, kissing her once more.

Cherry watched as Lobo quickly strode after her pa. Silently, she prayed for their safety—for their safe return. Black Jack had shot Pinky

Chitter, and Lobo was right: if he could turn on Pinky, he could turn on anybody in Blue Water. The folks in Blue Water weren't safe any longer. Someone had to dig the rot out of the town, and she knew there were only two men who had a chance at doing it.

A few minutes later, Cherry stood with Mrs. Blakely, Billy, and Griff—watching her pa and Lobo ride toward town. Everyone watched—watched until Lobo McCoy and Arthur Ray were out of sight, until their dust trails had settled. There was nothing to do but wait.

"Don't worry, Cherry," Billy said, placing a comforting arm around her shoulders. "Black Jack ain't got a chance against them two."

"Is that right?"

Cherry gasped when she heard his voice—heard the gunshot—saw Griff go down with one hand pressed to the bloody wound at his shoulder.

Spinning around, she held her breath—horrified at seeing Black Jack Haley standing behind them. Leveling his pistol at her, Jack chuckled and said, "Sweet Cherry Ray . . . now what kinda mischief have you been up to since I been gone?"

CHAPTER THIRTEEN

"Jack," Cherry breathed. All at once fear engulfed her! The day Black Jack Haley had chased her down—tried to force his vile intentions on her—all of it came flooding to the forefront of her mind. All the warnings Lobo had given her, all the times he'd told her that men like Jack could harm her if she wasn't careful—she knew the truth of it then. All at once her innocence of mind was shattered. The man standing in front of her was an outlaw—a murdering outlaw! He'd killed Texas Rangers, deputies—he'd killed the woman who had been loyal to him for years, the woman who'd loved him. All at once, Cherry knew the profound truth of everything Lobo had warned her about—of the true face of danger Black Jack Haley was.

Black Jack's greasy black hair was tucked behind his ears; the black of his britches and vest accentuated his ominous appearance.

"Mmmm mmmm!" Black Jack mumbled nodding his head with approval as he studied Cherry from head to toe. "My! Don't you look nice in that there blue dress."

"Leave her be," Billy growled.

"Billy Parker," Jack chuckled. "You growed a piece since I seen you last."

Griff moaned, and Mrs. Blakely carefully knelt down beside him. Jack glanced quickly at the old woman. "If'n yer wantin' to help that fool cowboy, then you hand me his iron, Mrs. Blakely," he said. "Slow and easy or I'll shoot the both of ya."

Mrs. Blakely didn't say a word. Slowly she drew Griff's gun from his holster and held it up to Jack. Cherry thought it was the only time she could remember Mrs. Blakely being so quiet.

Jack shoved Griff's gun into the back of his britches at the waist.

"Like I was sayin', Cherry Ray," he began, "don't you look nice."

"I said, you leave her be!" Billy growled once more.

Cherry gasped as the back of Jack's hand met Billy's cheek with brutal force.

"I do what I please, boy!" Jack shouted. "And I've always had my mind set to Cherry Ray."

"He'll drop you dead cold if you touch her," Billy said, wiping the blood from the corner of his mouth.

"Arthur Ray ain't dropped nobody in ten years, boy," Jack said. He smiled and struck Billy hard again.

"It ain't Arthur Ray I'm talkin' about."

"Billy," Cherry whispered. She shook her head—pleading with him to keep quiet. If

Black Jack had killed Pinky, Cherry was sure he wouldn't think twice about killing Billy.

"Do ya mean Lobo McCoy?" Jack asked.

"He'll drop you cold where you stand if you touch her," Billy answered.

Jack chuckled and looked at Cherry. "Pinky said you was sweet on that purty Ranger. What a shame," he said, shaking his head. "I hate to hafta kill a man as purty as I hear he is. Ain't enough purty boys in this world. Still, he's gunnin' for me . . . ain't he, Cherry? And since he's gunnin' for me, I'll hafta shoot him first."

"In the back . . . the way some coward in San Antonio shot his brother?" Cherry asked.

The back of his hand was hard against her tender cheek. The force of the blow knocked her to the ground.

"Cherry!" Mrs. Blakely cried. "Hush now! Don't provoke him any further!"

"I'll drop him whichever way I can," Jack snarled. "He didn't have no right to come into my town a-lookin' to gun fer me!"

"I've seen his draw," Cherry said, struggling to her feet. "And you ain't anywhere near fast enough."

"Even if he is faster than me—which he ain't—I ain't worried. 'Cause I got somethin' he wants."

Hot fear ran through Cherry's veins—the hair on the top of her head prickled.

Jack reached down, taking hold of her arm and yanking her to her feet.

"I got you," he said.

Cherry shook her head. Gritting her teeth, she growled, "I ain't goin' nowhere with you."

Black Jack Haley chuckled. "Yes ya are."

Cherry screamed as Jack pointed his gun at Billy and pulled the trigger! Billy Parker reeled back, stumbled, and fell against the porch steps.

"Billy!" Cherry cried. "Billy!" Struggling to break free of Jack's grip, she tried to get to Billy—to reach him before it was too late.

"I-I'm fine, Cherry," he said, holding his forearm. "I-I'm fine."

Mrs. Blakely's sobs were now audible.

"Shut yer mouth, old woman!" Jack shouted. "I'll kill him if ya sass me one more time, Cherry," Jack said, leveling his pistol at Billy once more. "Now, you come along with me . . . or I'll kill the boy."

"No, Cherry!" Mrs. Blakely whispered.

"I told you to shut yer mouth!" Jack said, lowering his gun at Mrs. Blakely.

"No! Don't!" Cherry cried. "I'll—I'll go. Whatever you want . . . just leave them alone."

Jack moved his pistol an inch and fired again, hitting Griff in the right leg.

"That's right . . . you will," Jack growled.

Cherry was sobbing, frightened beyond thinking! As Billy moved toward her, Cherry shook her head. "It'll be fine, Billy," she said. "It—it'll be just fine."

"Come on, girl," Jack said, pulling Cherry with him as he backed away. "If any of ya try to follow me . . . I'll kill her." Jack laughed and kissed Cherry's temple as he pulled her back against his body. "Now . . . let's get back to town so I can get a look at yer pretty little Texas Ranger. What do ya think he'll have to say when he sees I've got me a new girl?"

"He'll kill you," Cherry breathed. She winced as Jack twisted her arm behind her back.

"Oh, I'm afraid not, Cherry. I'm afraid that after today, you'll be buryin' yer purty Ranger—and yer pa—right out there in the boneyard with yer ma. Now come on!"

Cherry tried not to struggle. She looked over her shoulder to see Billy and Mrs. Blakely crouched over Griff.

"Now come on, Cherry," Jack said. "You don't want no more blood on yer hands."

"You're the one with blood on yer hands, Jack," Cherry sobbed. "Y-you murdered Pinky!"

"I didn't kill Pinky, Cherry Ray," Jack growled as he placed the barrel of his pistol to her back and nodded to his horse. "Lobo McCoy did!" Cherry put her foot in the stirrup and mounted Jack's horse. In a moment, he was mounted behind her. "Pinky didn't want me to gun down that purty Ranger of yers. She lied to me 'cause of him. I put the bullet in her chest . . . but it was yer Ranger that killed her."

Jack hollered, and his horse bolted into a full gallop. Tears streamed down Cherry's face; her mind twisted with fear and confusion. He'd use her—she knew. Black Jack Haley would use her to kill Lobo and her pa! Frantically, she tried to think of a way to escape. As the horse carried them toward Blue Water, Cherry Ray tried to think of a way to save Lobo and her pa—but there was nothing—nothing but terrifying fear and bitter, bitter despair.

She closed her eyes as they rode past the cherry tree her mother had planted. In her mind, she could see Lobo the day he'd been shot—see his smile only moments before the Baxter men had gunned him down. On her lips, she could almost feel his kiss—nearly sense his arms around her. Black Jack's breath on her neck ripped her from the daydream. Black Jack Haley was a coward—and Lobo McCoy wasn't. She knew Lobo would walk straight out in the street to meet Jack. She also knew Jack would be too cowardly to do the same. Jack intended to use her—to use Cherry to distract and dishearten Lobo. She thought about throwing herself off the horse, but she knew Jack would simply stop and force her to ride with him once more. She'd wait—wait until they got to town. Maybe then she could think—find a way to escape from Jack and save Lobo and her pa.

• • •

"Jack's boys are holed up in the saloon," Lobo told Arthur. "But there ain't no sign of Jack."

"Well, Pinky Chitter's laid out in Doc Milton's house . . . and sure as I'm standin' here, she's dead. So where's Jack?"

Lobo shook his head. "I don't know. . . . but I ain't waitin' around to get shot in the back. Let's have us a discussion with his boys."

Arthur nodded. He watched as Lobo fearlessly crossed the street toward the saloon. Lobo had a reason to finish what he came to Blue Water for. He knew Lobo's love of Cherry would give him a strength and determination—a strength and determination even his brother's death hadn't given him. Furthermore, Cherry would be cared for and loved—well cared for—obsessively loved. It made Arthur happy to think of Cherry and Lobo married, three or four little grandbabies running around in the pasture. He'd have to get rid of old Snort. That bull was too dangerous to keep when children were about.

With his own renewed determination, Arthur Ray crutched across the street behind Lobo McCoy. It was coming—the end of Black Jack's reign over Blue Water. Yes, indeed—it was coming.

Lobo walked through the saloon doors. He knew Arthur would make certain Jack didn't shoot him in the back. Arthur Ray was a tough old bird. Furthermore, he had his daughter in mind—her happiness. Lobo tried to push thoughts of Cherry from his consciousness. If he wanted her—wanted her for his own—then he had to finish what he'd come to Blue Water to start. Once Black Jack was in prison, Cherry could be his. He'd never known such powerful motivation.

"Where is he, boys?" Lobo asked as Fuss Ingram, Tucker Johnson, and Lee Taylor stood up from the table they'd been sitting at.

"Where's who, Ranger?" Fuss said.

"If you boys think he's gonna show you any more respect and loyalty than he did Pinky . . . you're dead wrong," Arthur said.

"Pinky did wrong by Jack," Fuss said.

"Is that so?" Lobo asked. "Well . . . I think Jack's turnin' a corner, boys. He's turnin' a corner, and he's gonna want to leave everybody else behind. Includin' you three boys."

"Jack won't turn on us," Lee said.

"I ain't gonna stand here and tell you boys what you already know," Lobo said. "I just want to know where he is. Fact is, I won't even drag you boys back to San Antonio—that is, if you tell me where Jack is and ride outta Blue Water right now. Give me Jack and you boys don't hafta go to prison . . . or die."

"Jack's gonna blow yer head wide open," Fuss said.

• • •

Arthur watched as Fuss Ingram drew on Lobo—but before the outlaw had cleared leather, he shouted when Lobo shot the gun from his hand.

Lee and Tucker put their hands on their guns but paused when Lobo said, "I'll drop you cold 'fore ya have a chance to finish drawin'."

Arthur smiled—delighted and awed by Lobo's speed and accuracy. He figured Lobo McCoy was faster than even he'd been in his prime.

"Coulda shot ya between the eyes just as easy, Fuss," Lobo said. "So tell me where Jack is."

Fuss swallowed. It was obvious he was rattled—still, his fear of Jack held strong.

"You can tell us now, Fuss . . . or you can stand there a-wonderin' if Jack can outdraw Lobo McCoy," Arthur said.

"Holster yer iron, Ranger," Fuss said. "Holster yer iron and . . . and I'll . . ."

"Jack will drop you dead, Fuss," Tucker interrupted.

"Ain't no way you can beat Jack, Ranger," Fuss said. "Not with what he's bringin' with him."

"It don't matter to me how many boys he's got ridin' in," Lobo said. "I'll drop him 'fore they drop me."

"It ain't that," Fuss said. Lobo heard a horse coming hard down the street, but he didn't turn. He didn't dare. Fear crept into his mind, trepidation washing over him as Jack's boys looked past him to the street outside the saloon—as Arthur Ray breathed, "Cherry!"

"Come on out, Lobo McCoy!" Jack shouted as he reined in the horse before the saloon. "I've got yer Sweet Cherry Ray here! She's hopin' to see ya one last time!"

Cherry wiped the tears from her cheeks as Jack dismounted, pulling her from the horse. Black Jack Haley would kill Lobo! He'd kill her pa too! She had to escape. She struggled as he took hold of her arm.

"Now, you don't want to die too . . . do ya, Cherry Ray?" Jack growled. "Come on! Yah!" he hollered, slapping his horse to send it galloping away. Jack pulled Cherry to stand in front of him and put the barrel of his pistol to her head. "Come on out, Ranger! You too, Arthur Ray. Get on out here!"

Cherry grimaced, sobbed as her pa crutched out of the saloon—as Lobo stepped out as well.

"Well, my, my, my," Jack chuckled. "You is one purty feller."

"You can go quiet back to San Antonio, Jack," Arthur began, "or you can go to yer grave with a bit more noise."

"I ain't goin' nowhere, old man." Jack cocked his pistol, and Cherry held her breath. "But she is—if'n you to don't put yer guns down."

Cherry looked to Lobo—saw the anger in his eyes—the anger and the fear.

"You shoot her and ya ain't got a chance," Lobo said. "Hidin' behind a woman," he added. "You ain't even got the courage to be a man and face me off proper."

"I got plenty a courage," Jack growled.

"Don't look like it from where we're standin', Jack," Arthur said. "It ain't no kinda man who'll shoot the woman that loves him. That there's a coward."

"You shut yer mouth!" Jack shouted suddenly. "She done me wrong! She done me wrong, and I give her what she deserved."

Cherry watched as Fuss Ingram, Tucker Johnson, and Lee Taylor slowly made their way out of the saloon and into the street. They stood behind Jack, and Cherry closed her eyes. Someone would die—her pa or Lobo. If she didn't do something, one or both of them would die.

"Face 'em like a man," she breathed. "You're a coward. I know it, your boys know it, and Pinky knew it."

"Shut up, Cherry!" Jack growled, moving the barrel of his gun from her head—pointing it at Lobo's. "Shut up!"

"Only a coward would hide behind me . . . provin' to the whole wide world that he is a coward!" she added.

He pushed her hard—threw her to the ground

with brutal force. And she thanked the Lord for the evil side of pride.

"All right, Ranger," Jack said. "We'll go around. We'll go around, and you'll die."

"Move, Cherry," Lobo growled. And she obeyed. Quickly she crawled out of the path of the men.

"But it's me and you, Ranger," Jack added, "Arthur Ray needs to drop his iron."

"Well, I would, Jack," Arthur said. "But, from where I'm standin', looks like yer boys ain't movin' off."

"Drop yer iron, Arthur . . . else Fuss'll shoot yer girl."

"Drop it, Mr. Ray," Lobo said. "It'll be fine."

Jack laughed. "You gonna face me and my boys alone, Ranger."

Lobo's eyes narrowed. "Way I figure it, there's only four of you . . . and I got five shots in my iron."

"Pa! No!" Cherry cried as she saw her pa slowly draw his weapon. He tossed it to the dirt and crutched to where Cherry now stood.

"Pa!" she cried. "Pa, you can't let him—"

"He'll be all right, Cherry," Arthur said. "He's right. He's got five shots and only four outlaws to drop."

Arthur smiled at Fuss Ingram when he frowned. Lobo McCoy was the fastest pistoleer he'd ever seen. Furthermore, Lobo was ready to finish his rangering days. Arthur was surprised by the peace washing over him. Black Jack Haley wouldn't go to prison. He wouldn't hang either. Black Jack Haley was about to be gunned down by a Texas Ranger.

"I'll give ya one more chance, Jack," Lobo said.

"Lobo!" Cherry whispered. "No!" Her pa held tightly to her arms. She couldn't believe her pa thought Lobo could talk Jack into going back to San Antonio to hang! Was he truly going to stand there and watch Lobo McCoy be gunned down?

"Drop yer iron and come on back to San Antonio," Lobo said. "Maybe the judge will go easy on ya."

"I ain't goin' back to San Antonio."

"What about yer boys? You gonna take them down with ya?"

"I'll take 'em down myself if they turn tail before I've dropped you, Ranger."

"You ain't faster than me, Jack," Lobo said. "I promise you this—yer a murderin' outlaw. And now . . . now you've threatened to harm my family. I ain't gonna let ya live. I'll shoot to kill before I let you live to kill again."

"He's awful fast, Jack," Fuss Ingram mumbled.

"Shut up, Fuss!" Jack shouted. "You know I'm faster!"

Cherry tried to breathe—tried not to faint.

The townsfolk in Blue Water lined the street on both sides now—watched from windows and held their breath. Lobo McCoy was about to be gunned down in Blue Water—and when he was, the town would be at the mercy of Black Jack Haley.

Tucker Johnson took a step backward, and Jack said, "If he don't kill ya, I will, Tucker." Tucker stopped, perspiration running over his face.

"You and me, Ranger," Jack said.

Lobo grinned. "If that's the way you want it, Jack. Then you just say when."

"Pa," Cherry whispered.

"He'll be fine, Cherry. He'll be fine. He's fightin' for a life with you. He'll be fine."

The sun blazed hot—the only sound was that of the breeze, a meadowlark's call, and its mate's answer.

Cherry watched—watched Black Jack's fingers poised above the grip of his gun. She gasped and screamed, "No!" as shots rang out.

It was over in an instant—in the time it took to draw a breath—Cherry Ray's life was changed forever.

She stood, breathless with horror—unable to move as she looked at the four dead men lying in the dirt. Glancing over to Lobo, she watched as he triggerguard-spun his pistol several times before holstering it.

No one moved—no one seemed to breathe.

"He done it, Mr. Ray. He really done it. I ain't never seen the like."

Cherry turned to see Billy Parker walking toward them. Blood stained his shirt sleeve, but he seemed unaffected, his gaze fixed on Lobo McCoy.

"How'd you get here, boy? And what in the world happened to ya?" Arthur asked.

"I rode Griff's horse," Billy said. "Mrs. Blakely's got Griff in the wagon. She's bringin' him in to see Doc Milton."

"What happened to Griff?" Arthur asked.

Cherry's heart began to beat with a different sort of rhythm—the rhythm a woman's heart beats when the man she loves is looking at her.

"Black Jack shot him," Cherry mumbled. "He shot Billy too."

Cherry felt goose bumps racing over her body—butterflies soaring in her stomach as Lobo starred at her—sauntered toward her. She was only slightly aware of the commotion that erupted around her—of her pa ordering Billy to Doc Milton's—hollering at the men in town to help him drag off the bodies of Black Jack Haley and his boys. She thought he may have told Mr. Hirsch to send a telegram to San Antonio. Still, she wasn't certain—for all that mattered in the world to her, all she could see, was Lobo—Lobo McCoy as he sauntered closer.

She felt a smile spread across her face as her

feet carried her toward him—as she ran toward him—as he caught her in his arms—gathered her against his strong body and kissed her.

"Lobo!" she breathed. "I—he—he—"

"Hush, darlin'. I don't want to think about all this no more today. Yer safe—and yer pa. That's all that matters to me." He kissed her again—moist affection drenching them both in passion. Cherry thought she heard Laura Parker, heard her gasp, heard Mrs. Parker tell her to quit watching such goings-on—but she didn't care. Lobo was safe! He was alive and safe, and he was going to belong to her.

"Marry me, Cherry?" he mumbled against her mouth. "Today—right now. I know it ain't very romantic—nothin' like Oklahoma Jenny and Sheriff Tate would do." He smiled at her—brushed a stray strand of hair from her cheek. "But I finished what I came to do and—"

"Yes!" Cherry exclaimed, throwing her arms around his neck. "I'll marry you today . . . this very minute!"

Lobo smiled and kissed her again. "I'm in mind we need the preacher." His warm brown eyes gazed into her blue ones. He loved her! She could see herself in his eyes, and he loved her. Her heart fluttered, beat fiercely as she realized that Lobo McCoy loved her as much as she loved him!

"Billy," Cherry said, turning to her young

friend. He'd obviously disobeyed her pa and still stood in awe instead of going to fetch Doc Milton. "Fetch the preacher after Doc Milton doctors up yer arm, will ya?"

Billy smiled, nodded, and said, "I'll fetch the preacher first!" He turned and ran off in search of the preacher.

Arthur smiled. The street would be cleaned up soon enough, and then he'd see to it—as soon as things settled down, he'd see that the preacher married Cherry and Lobo. The Baxter men who had shot Lobo could sit in the jailhouse a couple more days—as could Clarence Gibbs. He'd let the Rangers from San Antonio decide what do with them. For now, all he cared about was seeing Cherry and Lobo married.

"My little Sweet Cherry," he whispered, excess moisture filling his eyes. "Sweet Cherry Ray."

The evening was warm, and the pink- and lavender-colored clouds stretched out across the sunset sky as Lobo McCoy kicked the cabin door open. Carrying Cherry over the threshold, he let her feet drop to the dirt floor and gathered her in his arms.

His kiss was like pure confection. No more delicious thing existed on earth!

"This is the cabin Pa built when he first bought the ranch," Cherry began as he broke the seal of their lips for a moment, "before the big ranch house was put up."

"Mm hmmm," he mumbled, kissing her again.

He was hers—Lobo McCoy belonged to her! The preacher had married them only hours after Lobo had dropped Black Jack and his boys, and it seemed the wedding had served to heal the town of Blue Water—to give the townsfolk hope somehow. Now she stood in the cabin her pa and mother had lived in when they'd first been married—stood there with the man she loved—with the man who loved her.

"Wait here," he said, suddenly letting go of her. He turned and left the cabin, and Cherry smiled, puzzled. Several moments later, he returned.

"Where did ya go?"

Lobo smiled an alluring smile of mischief and held out one hand to her. In her excitement and bliss, Cherry had forgotten about the cherry tree her mother had planted next to the old cabin. There in Lobo's palm lay a handful of sweet cherries from the tree.

He took the stem off one of the cherries, tossed it high in the air, and caught it in his mouth a moment before pressing his lips to hers. Cherry's heart soared as he kissed her, and she giggled as she broke the seal of their lips, turned her head, and spit out the cherry pit she'd retrieved from Lobo's mouth during their kiss.

Tossing the remaining cherries onto the bed

setting against the wall nearby, Lobo pulled Cherry into his arms, gazing lovingly down into her face.

"I love you, Sweet Cherry Ray," Lobo breathed as his lips lingered a breath from her own.

"That would be Sweet Cherry McCoy," Cherry giggled. "And oh," she breathed, running her fingers through his hair, "oh, how I love you!"

And there, in the old cabin, as the sunset sent pink and lavender clouds to sleep, the legend of Sweet Cherry Ray and Lobo McCoy truly began.

EPILOGUE

Cherry closed the Oklahoma Jenny book she'd been reading. Smiling, she sighed—such pure contentment she'd never imagined. She giggled as Jefferson got to running faster than his little legs could keep up and tumbled into the sweet pasture grass beneath the cherry tree.

"Whoops!" she exclaimed, laughing with merriment as his little dark-haired head popped up and looked at her.

"I falled, Mama," he said, pushing himself to his feet once more. In an instant, he was off again—running in circles around the tree his grandmother had planted.

"You sure did," Cherry laughed.

The baby cooed, and Cherry smiled down at her. Jenny was growing so fast! She'd be crawling soon. Cherry shook her head as she smiled at the pretty baby lying on the blanket spread under the shade of the tree. If Jenny turned out to be as good at getting into mischief as Jefferson was, Cherry would never get a living thing done!

"Watch me, Mama! Watch! Watch!" Jefferson called.

"I'm watchin'!" Cherry assured him. Again, she giggled as she watched his little arms and legs pumping as he ran.

"Ain't I fast?" he asked.

"Mighty fast!"

Cherry gasped and held her breath as Jefferson plowed headlong into another tumble in the grass. He was up and smiling and off again soon enough, however, and Cherry sighed—tuckered out at just thinking about his endless activity.

Picking up a cherry that was lying nearby in the grass, Cherry McCoy rubbed it on her skirt and plopped it into her mouth. The cherries from her mother's tree seemed sweeter than ever, and she savored its delicious flavor.

"Daddy, Daddy! Daddy's comin', Mama!" Jefferson hollered as he took off running away from the tree.

"Jefferson McCoy!" Cherry scolded, catching hold of the waist of his little britches as he ran past her. "You wait right here! Daddy's ridin' fast, and you need to be careful. The horse might not see you."

Cherry smiled as the baby's arms and legs began wildly kicking with excitement. Both of Lobo McCoy's children knew when he was near. Cherry was always amazed at how they could sense him. Of course, Lobo said they were the same way about her—knew when she was returning from the garden after having been out awhile or coming back from picking things up in town.

Cherry let go of Jefferson's britches as Lobo reined up near the tree and dismounted.

"Daddy!" Jefferson hollered, running headlong for Lobo.

"There's my boy!" Lobo exclaimed, picking Jefferson up and lifting him high over his head for a moment before settling the toddler on his hip.

"I've been runnin' for Mama," Jefferson said, his little chest puffing out with pride.

"Oh, I bet ya have," Lobo chuckled, winking at Cherry. He sauntered over to where Cherry and the baby were, and Cherry smiled as the butterflies in her stomach took flight at the sight of him.

"Let me down, Daddy," Jefferson said. "And I'll do some good runnin' for ya!"

"All righty," Lobo said. "Get to it then. Let me see how fast ya are."

Cherry laughed, certain Jefferson's feet were already moving when Lobo set him down.

"And there he goes!" Lobo laughed, shaking his head.

"He's about to wear me out today," Cherry said as Lobo knelt down in the grass and kissed Jenny's soft forehead.

"I can see why," Lobo said.

"Do you wanna know what I caught him doin' today?" Cherry asked.

"I don't know . . . do I?" Lobo kissed Jenny again, and she smiled and began cooing.

"Feedin' ol' Snort sugar through the fence!"

she told him. "He poured sugar in his pockets and was lettin' that ol' bull lick the sugar off his hands!"

"That ol' bull sure takes to Jefferson," Lobo said, smiling as he stretched out on the grass beside Cherry.

"Oh, I know he ain't mean like he used to be ... but it still scares me, Lobo."

"Jefferson knows not to go past the fence, Cherry."

"I know . . . but I still worry."

Lobo smiled and chuckled. "That's called payin' for yer raisin', honey."

Cherry rolled her eyes and shook her head. She knew he was right, but it didn't make her worry any less.

"I checked in on yer pa while I was in town," Lobo said as Cherry handed him a couple of cherries.

"Is he feelin' better today?"

Lobo nodded. "Yep. I can tell his leg is botherin' him, but he was sittin' right there in the jailhouse jawin' with Remmy Cooper and Otis Hirsch. Looked as healthy as a horse."

Cherry still couldn't believe her pa had accepted the position of sheriff of Blue Water. It seemed so long ago that Black Jack Haley and his boys met their fatal end at the hand of Texas Ranger Lobo McCoy. She thought of the day soon after when her pa had told her he was sheriff of Blue

Water—that he was tired of ranching and wanted Lobo to run the ranch. It all seemed so long ago.

Cherry looked at Lobo—studied his handsome face. She thought of the old Mexican coin badge tucked in the bottom of the trunk in the parlor next to Ol' Red near the hearth, of the collection of bullets that had been dug out of Lobo's body at one time or the other lying in the trunk with the badge. Visions of Lobo riding into Blue Water and bathing in the creek leapt to the front of her mind. What an adventure it had all been!

Many were the times Cherry considered on how much more exciting and romantic her life had been than Oklahoma Jenny's. Lobo was the most wonderful man in the world! Kind, caring, compassionate, and yet more powerful and strong than any man Cherry had ever known, Lobo McCoy could do anything! Anything he set his mind to—including making Cherry's mouth water for wanting his kiss—simply by being close.

Cherry wondered if Oklahoma Jenny and Sheriff Tate had ever had children. They had finally gotten married in *Oklahoma Jenny—Bride of the West*, but it had been the last Oklahoma Jenny book published. Cherry shook her head, reminding herself that Oklahoma Jenny was a made-up character in a book, not a real person. Still, she wondered if they had children. She looked at her own—at Jefferson and Jenny—

and smiled. Pure contentment—that's what the moment was.

"I'm glad pa is happy," Cherry said. "I never thought bein' a lawman again would give him such gratification."

Lobo sighed. "Well, Blue Water needed a man who wasn't afraid of anythin'... and Arthur Ray sure ain't."

Cherry smiled and placed one palm on Lobo's cheek. He smiled, covered her hand with his own, and turned his head to kiss her palm. Goose bumps raced over Cherry's arms—she couldn't believe he was real, still couldn't believe he was hers. Lobo McCoy—her own!

"I saw Billy Parker in town today too," Lobo said.

"He and Susie Baxter still gettin' married at the end of the month?" Cherry asked. With her pa in prison, Susie Baxter's mother had taken hold hard of her boys—whipped them into fine young men. Susie was an angel, and Cherry was glad Billy Parker had finally taken notice of her.

"Yep... and movin' off to New York City." Lobo reached around to his back pocket and pulled out a book. "He gave me this... thought you might find it interesting."

Cherry frowned, puzzled as Lobo handed the book to her. As she turned the book over and read the title, she laughed. "Sweet Cherry Ray and Lobo McCoy!" she squealed. Indeed, the title of the book was *The Legend of Sweet Cherry Ray and Lobo McCoy*—the drawing in the front that of a woman closely resembling Cherry.

"By Billy Parker," Cherry whispered, shaking her head in disbelief.

Lobo smiled. "He says he didn't add nothin' . . . wrote it just the way it happened. 'Course now everybody knows what a spyin' little nosy rosy you are."

"I ain't spied a lick since I married you," Cherry said, leaning over and kissing him on the mouth. "Ain't a thing in this world worth spyin' on besides Lobo McCoy . . . and I can see him anytime I want." Cherry shook her head as she looked at the book again. "I can't believe it! That Billy Parker."

"It's somethin', ain't it?" Lobo chuckled.

Cherry looked at Lobo—leaned over and kissed him—giggled when he pulled her into his arms and rolled her over in the grass until he hovered above her.

"Sweet Cherry Ray," he mumbled as he studied her face—brushed a strand of hair from her forehead. "I still remember that first time I saw you—standin' there with yer pa and that ol' dried-up wolf."

"Well," Cherry said, smiling, "I always thought wolves were interestin'. Especially them handsome Texas Ranger types." She pushed his hat from his head and ran her fingers through his soft, dark hair.

"How can it be that I love you more every day?" Lobo mumbled.

"I love you more every day too," Cherry whispered as his head descended, his mouth capturing hers in a moist, demanding kiss. As always, goose bumps rippled over Cherry's body at the feel of her husband's arms around her—at the taste of his cherry-flavored kisses.

"Oh, stop that kissin'!" Jefferson exclaimed as he straddled Lobo's back. "I want to hear the new book ya brung, Daddy."

Lobo raised himself onto his hands and knees, and Cherry giggled as she watched him buck and twist like a green-broke horse. Jefferson held onto the back of Lobo's shirt, laughing with pure glee as his daddy finally managed to buck him off.

"So you wanna hear the new book I brung for yer mama . . . is that it?" Lobo asked.

Jefferson nodded. "I ranned for a long time . . . didn't I, Mama?"

Cherry nodded. He'd sure enough sleep well that night. She figured he'd been running rings around the old tree for near to an hour.

"You did do some runnin', that's for certain," Cherry said.

"Well, then I guess ya oughta be able to hear a bit of yer mama's new book," Lobo said. He stretched out on the grass beneath the tree, tucking his hands behind his head. Cherry laughed as she watched Jefferson study his daddy for a moment and then stretch out the same way next to him.

"We're ready, Mama," Jefferson said. "Jenny wants to listen too."

"All righty then," Cherry said. She picked up the book, shaking her head as she read the title to herself once more.

Lying down in the grass between Lobo and Jenny, she opened the book and began.

Cherry Ray stood and looked up to her pa, retired Texas Ranger Arthur Ray. Arthur's eyes were narrow, suspicious as he watched the stranger ride into town.

"Oh! This is gonna be a good one, Mama! I can tell," Jefferson exclaimed. "Keep goin'!"

Cherry smiled and read.

The stranger wore a black hat and pants the like of a Mexican cowboy. The silver buttons on his britches gleamed in the sunlight, and pretty Cherry Ray wondered why such a handsome stranger had come to Blue Water. It was the pistol at the stranger's hip, however, that caught Arthur Ray's attention. As the stranger rode closer and closer, no one spoke—the only sound was that of the breeze, a falcon's cry overhead, and the rhythm of the rider's horse as it slowed to a trot . . .

ABOUT THE AUTHOR

Marcia Lynn McClure's intoxicating succession of novels, novellas, and e-books—including *A Crimson Frost*, *The Visions of Ransom Lake*, *The Bewitching of Amoretta Ipswich* and *Midnight Masquerade*—has established her as one of the most favored and engaging authors of true romance. Her unprecedented forte in weaving captivating stories of western, medieval, regency, and contemporary amour void of brusque intimacy has earned her the title "The Queen of Kissing."

Marcia, who was born in Albuquerque, New Mexico, has spent her life intrigued with people, history, love, and romance. A wife, mother, grandmother, family historian, poet, and author, Marcia Lynn McClure spins her tales of splendor for the sake of offering respite through the beauty, mirth, and delight of a worthwhile and wonderful story.

Center Point Large Print
600 Brooks Road / PO Box 1
Thorndike, ME 04986-0001 USA

(207) 568-3717

US & Canada:
1 800 929-9108
www.centerpointlargeprint.com